SLIPPERY GLASS

The Laws of Sowing and Reaping

by

EPIC SKY JACKSON

EPIC ENDEAVORS 2

ISBN: 978-0-578-62967-4

Printed in the United States of America

DEDICATION

This book and the struggles I had to overcome
to accomplish such great works are dedicated
to my two beautiful and loving daughters.

I would like to also dedicate this book
to my sister who raised me from the age of 6,
who has always been the wind beneath my wings.

A WORD FROM THE AUTHOR

I HAD TO LEARN TO TRUST GOD'S PROCESS... unsure how life's short comings, difficulties and set backs was going to eventually mold me in such a way that they weren't no longer seen as a negative. But seen as an important factor for my mental and spiritual growth that was going to be needed as I continue my journey. I was resilient in my purpose, the people who know me as a friendly smile that takes a delight in my work and to the people whom have gotten the privilege of knowing me personally. Even with all the love support and positive energy I try to surround myself with, people can be dangerous, this is the reality of success. Some people will purposely put stumbling blocks in your path and when that is no longer working they will use mountains. Mountains are situations that's a person's personal fears rather it's defeat, finances, or setbacks. It exists and it's real. I've met some wonderful and beautiful people on my journey. I also have met the ugly. I've found myself asking my God despite the changing faces and whatever he have me to go through to stay close to me. No matter what struggles that may be ahead, let not my sacrifices have not been in vein. Many have lost their way on this path.

Some may want you to keep your dreams silent, because it makes them feel uncomfortable. I tell you speak the Glory of God to the world of your blessful gift. There are people God have purposedly designed a date and a destinated time you will cross path with them. This moment was designed by God to compliment your journey.

If you fall, let me let you know right now. My best advice is to give yourself CPR, because no one is coming to breathe Purpose, Will, and Hope back into you. Your dreams will lay right down next to you and they will die with you too.

The human spirit will to survive is much more powerful than we speak of. It's an unspeakable transformation within oneself.

But PASSION, she will wake you up within the morning hours. She will toss thoughts inside your head, until it becomes imperative to find pen, pencil, paper, even a paper bag, the palms of my hands if needed to jot down her thoughts. SEE PASSION, she will find a way to RISE through personal, player haters tricks, preset circumstances, life! You know what she tells me, it comes a time in life SELF PRESERVATION must be the concrete floor for your dreams. I asked what is your name, she said I'm the CONSCIOUS of DESIRE My name is PUSH!!!!!!

The characters of Slippery Glass are calling me to write their continuing story. Watch for the sequel *Hades*.

CHAPTER 1

On a crowded beach on a hot summer day, Dedrick Mercandel, a 5'8" African-American man in his mid 50s, disguised as a homeless person to allow him to fit in among the many homeless people on the side of the boardwalk. He drinks from a flask as he watches three people ride jet skis and two women on a sailboat. A boat is docked at a distance. He sees three well-dressed Jamaican men walking by loading their guns. One of the men has his eyes fixated on a very large yacht sitting about a mile from shore. "Those dirty Columbian bastards think that they going to give us what they want to give us, we going to take all they shit." The man as he walks past Mercandel's leg kicks it and continues to walk on nonchalantly.

The other Jamaican man spits on the ground near Mercandel's feet. He stops in front of Mercandel's feet which were extended out, saying, "Move your leg you old dirty piece of shit!" He takes out his gun and points it at Mercandel's feet, "Before I blow both of those mutherfuckers off." Mercandel slowly reaches his hand out and moved one foot at a time back never breaking eye contact with the man. The three Jamaicans continue to walk onto the boardwalk toward the docked boats.

Mercandel picks up a pocket spy micro key and taps it. He watches the three men as they head toward board the small yacht.

On the large yacht there are four Columbian men sitting down laughing, talking and drinking scotch. There is a briefcase on the table and a small black transceiver. Jonathan, a Cuban man in his mid 30s, notices the transceiver receiving a message. He reaches for the box and reads the message. His brother Christopher, a young man in his mid 20s, focuses on Jonathan. Jonathan looks at Christopher, "It's a dead deal."

Christopher turns around slowly, "It can't be!" Then he stands up and glancing at the other men, "We've been doing business with them for years, this is bullshit."

Jonathan watches the transceiver closely listening. Everyone in the room is very quiet and nervous. Christopher walks closer and leans over to Jonathan. "Brother! Father will not have us travel this far to turn back now with two hundred keys."

Jonathan drops the box on the floor. He turned to Christopher angrily, "You idiot, he wouldn't have asked us to come this far to get killed or put underneath an American jail!"

Jonathan rushes over to a nearby window. He sees the

three jet skis and the sailboat with the two women on it. Jonathan is still looking out the window nervously, "Ricky! Ricky!"

Ricky the boat's captain, runs into the room looking around frantically, "Sir?"

Jonathan turns around and looks at Ricky straight in his eyes and points his finger into Ricky's face, "Listen to me and listen to me fucking clearly. Start moving this boat out nice and slow. Don't draw no attention from the harbor patrol you will encounter to your left ten miles out."

Ricky attempts to walk off, Jonathan stands there watching him with a blank look, "Ricky." Ricky turns around fearfully and looks at Jonathan. "If this boat gets stopped, I will have your body cut in pieces before they even board and I will hand it over to them on a plate."

Ricky begins to tremble in his voice, "Yes sir." Ricky rushes out the room almost tripping over his own feet.

Jonathan gazes out a nearby window, then turns suddenly and looks at Christopher. "How in the hell can you put so much trust in a man you never saw or touched before?"

Christopher looks at Jonathan modestly, "because our father trusts him. Once every five years for the last twenty years, no losses, no mistakes. Who really cares who he is Jonathan, does it really matter? Some things are better left alone."

On the Beach, children run pass and people are walking around having fun. One of the Jamaican men sees the Colombian yacht moving slowly out into the open water, "What the Fuck." The other two Jamaican men turn their attention on the Columbian yacht. moving. Suddenly, all three men begin to walk quickly, trying not to draw any attention. The Jamaicans rush onto their own small yacht and gradually the boat begins to move.

Slowly, Mercandel stands up, pulling a very small detonator from his pocket. As he watches the Jamaican yacht pull out and pick up speed, he presses a button and the yacht explodes!

Chaos erupts on the beach as people stop and look at the yacht blown to pieces in fear and begin running and screaming. A homeless man standing next to Mercandel looking at the explosion, "I'd rather be broke and alive than rich and dead."

Mercandel also still looking at the explosion, "I prefer rich and alive." He walks off. As he walks pass a trash can, he drops the detonator in the trash without stopping or looking back.

Jonathan is on the back of the boat with Christopher looking at the explosion. He turns and looks at Jonathan, "Who cares what he looks like? To our family, he is like a God. He is priceless! Brother."

Christopher picks up a glass of wine, "What if he ever fell off? Can we trust a man with no face, no identity?"

Jonathan picks up a bottle of wine and begins to pour himself a glass. As he is pouring the glass of wine never looking up at Christopher, "Falling off is never an option, remember that lil brother." Jonathan walks off sipping a glass of wine. We are Colombians from the blood, from the follicles of our hair to the bareness of our feet.

CHAPTER 2

It's a beautiful day in Venice Beach, California. As Mercandel enters a coffee shop he sees a cell phone on a nearby table next to a laptop. He walks over to the counter. There are people drinking coffee and moving around. The Cashier standing at the counter asks, "May I help you?" Mercandel is standing there with his eyes closed and then suddenly opens them. "I would like to have a Grande Americano with an extra shot please." The Cashier walks away. She comes back to the counter and Mercandel is gone, but there is a twenty-dollar bill laying on the counter.

Mercandel is walking down the boardwalk toward the beach. He changes out the sim card in the cell phone from the coffee shop. He dials a number and pulls headphones with a mic from his pocket putting them in his ears as he walks. Mercandel speaks into the phone, "I'm resigning, no strings attached. I'm stepping out."

Lopez responds, "But you have been so good to me and my organization over the years. Do you want more money? Whatever you want Bishop."

Mercandel smiles and responds, "My children are older, and a smart man gets out before he gets wrapped up in the caught up."

Lopez responds, "I never met you, but you have been loyal to me like family. Matter of a fact it's more purified than just family. Because even family test their loyalty."

Mercandel responds, "That works better on your end than on mine."

Lopez takes a sip of his wine with a blank look on his face, "Ok, nice working with you my friend."

Mercandel responds, "Same here." Then he hangs up the phone, unplugs headphones and throws the phone in the ocean and walks off.

Lopez looks at his son bewildered, "he's so so so 'Cold'."

Rodrigo, a dangerous looking thug in his mid 40s, stands nearby. Jonathan stands up, looks out the window, and leans against the wall with a glass of wine in his hands. Christopher enters and stops when he sees Jonathan smiling at him. Jonathan, smiling wickedly, "Hi my dear, sweet brother."

Christopher gives Jonathan a dirty look, then takes a seat in front of Lopez's desk. Lopez turns around. Christopher looks at his father who has a frozen look on his face. "What's wrong Father?"

Lopez responds, "Bishop called me, telling me he's

resigning." Jonathan laughs while Lopez hits the wall with his fist with a loud BANG!

Jonathan looks at Christopher angrily, "BISHOP. We have to call him Bishop because no one knows his fucking name and we have paid this man millions of dollars."

Christopher looks back at his father and Jonathan in confusion, "He did the job. His name wasn't important then. What is the point now?"

Lopez POUNDS his fist on the desk, then looks at Jonathan. Jonathan nods his head in acceptance on his decision with a smirk on his face.

The Butler knocks on the halfway open door and then proceeds to walk into the room. Lopez takes a sharp paper sticker. He gets up and grabs the Butler by the front of his shirt and began stabbing him in the chest repeatedly over and over again. Lopez whispers in the Butler's ear as his head lay lifeless sideways. "Don't you ever just knock and walk into my domain without my permission, ever again." He takes his hand off his shirt and the Butler falls lifelessly to the floor. Christopher turns his head. Johnathan laughs underneath his breath while staring at Christopher.

Lopez goes and sits back at his desk, "Because I'm disappointed and angry."

Christopher, "What did he do wrong, father?"

Lopez begins to wipe his hands off on a handkerchief on his desk, "I was just thinking about that Christopher. I couldn't find a reason. I just want him dead and I want him dead today. Christopher puts his head down for a moment, then looks off. Lopez looks at Christopher, "You have a problem Christopher?"

Christopher looks at Lopez, "No sir."

Lopez sits down and gazes out his big window, "It took me years, I mean years to uncover him. I was hoping this day would never come. But it has, and I must take him down." He looks over at Rodrigo and nods. Rodrigo acknowledges him, then leaves the room. Christopher and Jonathan look at each other gravely.

CHAPTER 3

While Mercandel is vacationing in Africa with his sons, he sees a small girl about the age of 7 in a ragged dress and bare feet eating off the ground. Mercandel walks up beside her and she raises up and smiles. She offers her hand out to share her cookie. Mercandel looks down at her with a sadden smile. He takes the cookie and puts it in his pocket. He tells her, "Your smile is as beautiful as the skies. I will name you Sky." Mercandel reaches down and picks the child up.

She asks, speaking in her native tongue Swahili, "Where are you taking me?"

Mercandel speaking in Swahili asks her "Where are your parents."

She answers sadly, "They are dead."

Mercandel stops and he looks at her with a straight look, then he smiles. He tells her, "I will take care of you."

Sky gives him a big hug and begins to cry.

Dante and Derrick walk up with shopping bags to their father looking at him strangely. Mercandel tells them, "You now have a little sister, your mother has been wanting a little girl."

The two boys look at each other and smile, "Are you serious Father."

Mercandel, "Yes, she will stay here in a boarding school in Africa to learn her etiquette and teachings. We will come here every three months until she is ready to be brought to America. Then we will come back and get her and introduce her to your mother."

Dante responds, "We have a little sister. You are just so cool Father, how you just figure things out. They actually are miraculous the things you come up with."

Derrick takes a shirt out his bag and walks over to a flowing water fountain. Then looks over at Sky as she is still hugging Mercandel while cautiously watching the boys. Derrick wets the shirt and walks back to Mercandel and gently wipes her feet and the dirt off of her face with a smile. She smiles back at Derrick.

CHAPTER 4

Meanwhile back in the States, a meeting is being held In Lieutenant Watkins' office at the police station. Later that evening, Combs is called into Lieutenant Watkins' office. A nervous Combs, fidgeting nervously, sits in a chair as Lieutenant Watkins storms into the room slamming the door behind him. He throws snapshots of Mercandel and his sons shooting at the range on the desk. Lieutenant Watkins simmering angrily asks, "What in the hell is this, Combs?"

Combs opens his mouth to say something when Lieutenant Watkins holding his hand up to silence him continues, "First of all, before you say a word, other detectives that have earned great merits have turned down this investigation because of the shame of failing to catch Mercandel. What the fuck! He's the Colombians' and the Mafia's most precious stock. Do you want them to blow up the whole fucking police station with us inside this mutherfucker?"

Lieutenant Watkins lights a cigarette, rises with his

back turned to Detective Combs and gazes out the window. Detective Combs, "Sir, he's training his sons for his own militia."

Lieutenant Watkins smirks, "No, Combs, he is his own militia." Lieutenant Watkins, taking a deep breath continues, "This one man educates himself on his enemy. His perfect appearance on any day would be mistaken for a stockbroker on Wall Street. But he's notorious with knowledge." He sighs.

Continuing on, Lieutenant Watkins utters, "Yeah...I know Mercandel from way back. I had a case of conviction against him. One hundred thousand dollars of pure heroin, straight connection from Cuba. He opened up just days before a foreign car dealership. In the large crates, there were supposedly six Lamborghinis, an unexpected shipment. We thought we had his black ass. He fixed it where the cars were a cover-up, for the drugs. Later on, we found an abandoned ship fifty miles up the coast which was carrying the dope."

Lieutenant Watkins turns around, sits down to face Combs. Lieutenant Watkins, "Somehow, that innocent face of his manipulated the jury into believing that he was just waiting at the dock to verify his shipment...that he was innocent as a newborn baby.

I saw this man in the courtroom with my very own eyes, coach his top of the line lawyer how to win the case. The lawyer walks into the courtroom with his briefcase, Mercandel follows close behind him. Back then, he even intimidated me. Even though I knew the case was solid. We had the pictures, fingerprints, and at the same time, he walked out with a mistrial He used the system. I wake up every day to serve and protect. The entire situation was a set up. He let us put all our attention on him knowing that he already had a well thought out plan, so that the other hundreds of thousands of dollars of heroin could get in. Clever! Isn't he? I could have lost my entire career on a mishap."

Lieutenant Watkins leans forward closer to Combs. He whispers. "You know what Combs, just like you, I wanted him too! It's an insult to let him to hustle the streets playing Russian Roulette."

Detective Combs is becoming irate, "He's still a fucking dope dealer, no matter how you try to slice it up!"

Lieutenant Watkins looks away for a moment then glances back at Detective Combs. There is a miniature chess game sitting on his desk. He takes all the pieces off the game board. He picks up two chess pieces and places them one on top of the other. He points at the top one, "This one represents the Mafia and the Colombians." He then points at the second piece, Lieutenant Watkins trembling as he states, "This is the brilliant one, their God, best friend, mother, father, children, religion. He's their GOD!"

Lieutenant Watkins, quietly staring at Combs for a moment, "Are you listening to me! He's the one the Mafia and the Colombians use to mastermind the trafficking for the big dope. From every second to the minute to the hour, he knows the perimeter of every inch to the miles outside of the perimeter." He laughs. "Even how the air is circulating, weather forecast on that day, you will never see him. We spent years investigating this man and we still came up with nothing to catch him." Pausing, "This man or whatever the hell you want to call him, has his identity sealed. It's amazing, isn't it? We can catch the dealer and the supplier, but never catch the illustrator of the blueprint.

"Detective Combs, tell me you're kicking me in the ass right now. It would feel much better than you trying to make me believe you're not and you really are. If you're sitting here telling me that there is someone that is human, bleeds red blood..." He then screams, "that the Colombians and the Mafia can't do without him to push dope into the United States." Lowering his tone, "An American, and no one can catch him? So, what the fuck! Is he a fucking terrorist?"

Lieutenant Watkins continues, "He owns an entire luxury sport car dealership. He can also account for every penny in his bank account. He may have a million accounts. We only know about that one." Lieutenant Watkins, smiling, "He's clever...so clever."

Detective Combs says with a confused and angry look

on his face, "So, we are just going to let him just ship drugs into the United States like it's sugar or grain and not do anything?" Combs, his face turning purple in anger, yells, "Look at these pictures! He has sons, they're young, they're smart, they have extreme marksmanship and Dedrick Mercandel is their father. They've been training to shoot since they were four, since their hands were strong enough to hold a gun."

Lieutenant Watkins, "What is the case against the boys? They are on the honor roll at school. They never made a B in their lives. Chess is their expertise. This is America, you can't just go picking up people without any evidence." Detective Combs angrily jumps up and slams his fist on Lieutenant Watkins' desk. Watkins tells Combs, "I'm taking you off the Mercandel case. You're going to have our backs up against the wall once again with the same suspect. He knows the system."

Detective Combs, "I can serve him his warrant without any fatalities. But you know that's bullshit! How are you going to let one man contradict the law? One man! Oh my God!"

Lieutenant Watkins, stressing, "We are the law. No matter what, we must follow rules and regulations. I see you throwing the last fifteen years of your career down the drain..." Watkins yelling as he continues, "behind one man! I've never seen a man not sweat for his own life. Have you?"

Detective Combs straightens his composure and takes two deep breaths, "Well Sir, I do respect your authority and I apologize for getting too overwhelmed with this case, and I hope it hasn't reflected or discredited my character."

As Detective Combs strolls toward the door. Lieutenant Watkins emphasizes, "He has become the system. So therefore, we must wait until he slips." Sternly looking at Combs, he states, "You better believe that he already knows you have taken pictures, and that he has been under surveillance. Let me remind you that back then, he couldn't be underestimated. Now ten years later, he has no limitations. Combs, what I'm doing is for the best interests of your career. We will resurface an investigation on him once I return from vacation. Don't do anything stupid while I'm gone.

Detective Combs STORMS OFF never looking back, muttering, "Whatever! One fucking man!" He SLAMS the door behind him.

Lieutenant Watkins stands for a moment in bewilderment. He whispers to himself, "Yes Combs...one fucking man!"

CHAPTER 5

A few days later, standing outside the police station as evening approaches, Combs is directing the officers he assigned to the case to check their firearms. As Detective Combs approaches them snapping on his bullet-proof jacket; one of the officers states, "Detective Combs, there are four children involved in this investigation. We will be serving their father a Warrant in a matter of 24 to 48 hours. It can turn instantly into a hostile situation."

Detective Combs answers, "Can a child kill if they have a gun? Besides, these are not kids. They are young men, sixteen, seventeen, and a set of eighteen-year old twins. Did you see their pointers on the shooting range? They didn't miss one shot."

Detective Combs, turning to the other officers declares, "There are no one on this police force that has ever hit the pointers like these young men" A second officer asserts, "But Sir, there's nothing on these young men. Why are they suspects?" I'm sure you know that these boys are not going to let you just walk into their domain and take their father.

Combs, walking closer to the second officer, then leans into his face, talking very slowly to be sure he got the message as he exclaimed, "They are professional marksmen! In six months, we're going to have snipers! What part did you miss?"

Combs angrily looking back and forth at the officers, "Do you think they are doing this as a damn hobby? Men train for years and have never been this perfect. Do you think it's a joke? We're setting up the base in the hills about ten to fifteen seconds from the target." He points at the middle of the officer's head as he states, "They can shoot you here, right here from five blocks away. That doesn't sound like children to me. It sounds like Mercandel hasn't been in the spotlight for a couple of years. But now he has resurfaced with his own personal militia." As the rest of the policemen view the pictures, they are in total disbelief.

CHAPTER 6

Dedrick Mercandel picks up the boys for their weekly trip to the firing range. As the boys are getting into the car, Dedrick puts on his smooth special designer Versace glasses. The boys, Rico, Dedrick, Jr. and Travis sit in the back seat and Dante sits in the passenger seat.

They begin to drive off. Rico announces, "Father, I will be receiving a full scholarship in Law. I will be graduating at the top of my class."

Dedrick, "Son, that reminds me, your mother has some mail for you from some of the top colleges in the United States. It's in the mail bin at home. We wanted to surprise you." Dante gazes out the window disgusted. Rico continuing, "Father, this is my future, and even though they are my teachers, I always take a personal interest to inquire about my academics."

Dante turns around and gives Rico a dirty look. Then he turns back around in his seat and glances for a moment at his father. Dante, sullenly, "Well, Father, since my twin wants to bring up academics like he didn't know, and besides us being in the same class, I had an incomplete on my essay. Dante turns and peers out the window.

Dedrick gazes at Dante for a moment. Then he looks ahead and continues to drive along. "Dante, your brother Rico is speaking on his own behalf."

Dedrick peers at the other boys in the backseat through the rear-view mirror. He raises his voice, "You know what sons, your gift of breathing, intelligence, strength, endurance through weakness..." He pauses mid-sentence, then smiles. "Don't take it personal. Your mother and I will love all of you, whether you're bums in the street, or the President of the United States. Your gift of having just a chance to live is your gift from God. Every day you wake up is a battle. Maybe no man in our house hasn't fallen yet, but every couple of minutes, some man has fallen and given up somewhere."

Dedrick balls up his fist as he drives and presses it on the dashboard. "Now, we are the trunk." He tightens his fist. Dedrick continuing, "You see the strength I'm putting into my life?" Slowly opening his fist like a flower blossoming, "Our family represents the leaves." Moments later they arrive at the firing range. Dedrick pulls up and parks in front. The boys jump out of the Land Rover with their own personal rifles and gun cases.

A man in his late 60s smoking a cigar greets them. He is Billy, a humble Caucasian man, who has been their trainer from the beginning. Smiling as he hands the boys their earplugs, "Hello boys. How are you today?" They respond, "Good Morning, Sir." grabbing their earplugs as they head to the firing range.

With their father only steps behind them, the boys rush off to find the perfect stall to start their practice course. They all begin shooting the target at the same time ending with the same shot simultaneously. The other customers stop shooting to watch the boys shoot. Not skipping a beat, Billy strolls along with Mercandel to join his sons. Dedrick with a proud look on his face states that the boys will try out for the shooting tournament.

Billy, laughing exclaims "They are too damn good! They are going to have to go against men who are twice their age."

Dedrick asks, "Then what's the problem? It's a challenge. A man that's afraid of a challenge is a weak man. I'm raising men." Dedrick chuckling, "Their nuts are hanging too low to be called boys." Billy and Dedrick laugh as they watch the boys flatter themselves with their expertise in shooting.

With a serious look on his face, Billy asks, " So Mercandel, your sons are very intelligent, skillful, and respectful. What do they want to be when they graduate from high school?

Dedrick pauses for a minute in deep thought. He smiles, "I have made it possible for my sons to be whatever and whoever they choose to be. They do not know what it's like not to have, but they know how to get any and everything they want or feel they deserve." He continues, "Before long, the black man is going to be extinct. I taught them that knowledge is power. Read, read, read, and read some more. My sons have never lived or dealt in the streets. All four of them were born with silver spoons in their mouths with their names on them. But believe me, they are not scared of the streets. Every man should teach his sons survival instincts."

Billy comments "I hope I'm still around when they take their roles in life. They're going to make you a proud father, one of these days. I have watched all of them grow up. Not one time did they ever doubt you."

Thoughtfully Dedrick states, "Well, there hasn't been one time I disappointed them, without an explanation. Now they give me the same respect. I tell my sons that if your intellect, attire, and posture are on cue, your presence without speaking a word will speak for itself." Laughing, Billy shakes his head with acceptance of Dedrick's speech.

Billy, reflecting "You know Mercandel, there hasn't been one time since these boys have come to this shooting range on Saturdays and played paint sport in the fields, that they didn't check their guns at least twice before loading in the paint cartridge. Over the years, I have seen many young boys. I can honestly say, that you've been on your job to make sure the welfare of the children's safety has always been top priority.

Dedrick replies, "They are my priority!"

The boys' training ends. They hop into the Land Rover. Billy walking Dedrick halfway to the Land Rover asks, "So, are you guys going to the fight tonight?"

Dedrick says "No, I asked them...they weren't interested. But tonight is our family meeting. They look forward to family time once a week. I'm sure they have a lot of proposals already written down."

Billy pats Dedrick on his back, "Alrighty Mercandel, you and your family have a safe evening." Dedrick drives off. Billy stands there and watches as they drive off.

CHAPTER 7

The sunlight reflects on the family picture from the large bay window in Mercandel Mansion. You can hear laughter from a woman and man. Mercandel sits at the table drinking coffee with his wife, Linda, a woman of extraordinary beauty. They are discussing his traveling all over the world in his job as a consultant. He is telling her he is tired of all of the traveling and wants to stay home with her and the boys. She asks, "Are you sure you want to quit?"

Mercandel responds, "I am. Thought long and hard. Just want to be here with you and the boys."

Linda gives Mercandel a smirk, "I'm glad." She takes his hands, sits on his lap, kisses him deeply. "I love you."

Mercandel returns the kiss "I love you too. You're my reason. Don't forget that."

Heavy footsteps are heard. BANG! The door SLAMS. Linda stands abruptly and reaches her arms out to greet her sons with the warmest hug a mother could give. Dante, Rico, Travis, and Derrick are all on cue, from their perfect haircuts and tailored clothing all the way to the spotless patent leather shoes. Travis walks over to his father with a blunt look on his face.

Mercandel looking Travis directly in his eyes. "Son, was there a problem at school today that you and your brothers couldn't handle?" Mercandel looks at his other sons. They look at Mercandel with blank looks on their faces.

Linda, concerned, "Darling, what's wrong?" Dante, Rico, and Derrick look at each other, then hurry out of the kitchen.

Mercandel stands, "Speak, a man should be able to express his feelings but not move on them. Right now, you are moving in your feelings and that's disturbing. In other words, I'm telling you the World will eat your ass alive wearing your dam emotions on your chest. What part you not understanding. The Only People that love you..." Mercandel points up "First God, then Your mother and father. "

Travis cuts Mercandel off, "I didn't make the football team."

Mercandel walks off, bursts into LAUGHTER, and then turns around looking at Travis with a smirk. "What the hell!!! So what? The world is not going to stop turning until you catch up. The sun will rise and set tomorrow with or without you playing football.

First of all, a dog! A dog! The animal we train. Which is beneath a man? If you deny him food; Now even though you own that dog, and nursed that dog, that same dog will find a way to jump that fence or dig himself a hole to get out. Freedom and peace are choices. Please, son, do not underestimate your intelligence. I didn't have a litter, I have strong, intelligent young men as sons. Dedrick points his finger at Travis' chest. Travis is saddened.

Linda walks over and gives Travis a kiss of comfort. "Travis, you are talented in swimming and basketball. You even won the state championship in chess...it's not the end of the world."

Travis responds, "It's not just football Mother. I want to play professional football."

Mercandel smirks looks around then looks back at Travis. He says "Son, all I can tell you is try harder next year. You did your best. If you feel your best wasn't good enough, then you train harder. Get over it. Man up, Travis, does your Mother need to buy you maxi pads. You're better than that." Travis began to walk off angrily.

Linda looks at Mercandel with a blank look, "Dedrick, he's hurting."

Mercandel looks at Travis, "Son, did you ask permission to be excused? Because I don't recall you saying anything, and you sure in the hell didn't hear a word from your Mother and I."

Travis stops suddenly in his tracks. He turns around and faces his parents. Travis is very upset and tries to hold his feelings in, "May I please be excused?"

Mercandel still looking at Travis, "Linda, would you like to tell Travis anything else? Because he has nothing but time to listen, at least as long as he is under my roof."

Linda gives Travis a hug and then steps back holding both of his hands, "Travis, God has blessed you with many talents."

Travis is teary, "Is that it?"

Mercandel strolls over to Travis, sizes him up. He straightens out his son's shirt collar. Mercandel smiles at Travis, "All I have to say is I love you son. You are my son I raised and molded. If you enter in the game feeling inferior, you will be the inferior. Start training now for next year. The world was not built in one day. If you know otherwise, then you need to let me know. What did you think? That you were going to wake up one day and say, 'Today I want to be a football player!' Work harder or give up. The choice is yours."

Travis just glares. Mercandel rubs Travis' head with one stroke of his hands gently, "You're excused."

Travis walks off. Linda walks over to Mercandel and gives him a kiss and hugs him around the waist. Linda looks at Mercandel with concern, "He needed comfort."

Mercandel looks at Linda, "Linda, don't get comfort confused with sympathy. The world will not comfort them, and if they go into the world looking for comfort as men, the world will conquer them."

Linda paused and becomes upset, "Well, they are my babies and they are my world, and I will not conquer them."

Mercandel kisses Linda and picks her up as she screams with laughter. Mercandel, "You're right...as always." He sets her on the table and kisses her again.

He heads over to the staircase. Travis is sitting there with his head in his hands. "You ready to start now?"

Travis looking confused, "What?"

Mercandel looks up the stairs calling, "Derrick, Rico, Dante! We have a man down. What do we do when one of us is wounded?"

Travis replies, "We step up."

Mercandel proudly looking at Travis, "That's right." The other boys appear at the top of the stairs. Mercandel looks up, "Get a football and let's go. We have work to do." Travis smiles. Mercandel and Travis lead the boys outside. Linda smiles, she loves them so much it hurts.

◆ ◆ ◆

Outside of the Mercandel mansion a slim Columbian

stands in the darkness of the bushes. Rodrigo, Lopez's hit man, sits in a big black SUV smoking a cigarette. An unmarked police car pulls up next to him.

Detective Combs gets out and approaches Rodrigo. "Rodrigo, you got something for me?" Rodrigo hands him an envelope. Combs looks in it. It's stuffed with cash. Combs looks back at Rodrigo, "Pleasure doing business with you."

Rodrigo looks at Combs as he starts to walk off, "just do it." They glare at each other, then Combs gets back in his car and drives away. Rodrigo responds, "Pende-jo."

In the kitchen of Mercandel's home Dante, Derrick, and Dante pass through excited while Travis lingers behind. Mercandel playfully puts Travis in a choke hold.

Travis is laughing loudly, "Come on Dad, that's not fair. You caught me from behind."

Mercandel steadily playing with Travis "And that's why a wise man never sits with his back to the door. Always look from the corner of your eyes, observe everything and everyone."

Travis wrestles himself away from Mercandel. He then gives his father a fake left and right before running off to join his brothers outside.

Linda and Mercandel stroll off hugging each other. In the back of Mercandel's home is about a dozen cops in position hiding behind trees. Detective Combs is hovering over the officer who is laying on the ground holding a Remington M24 Sniper Weapon System with a scope. Combs is sweating as he watches Mercandel's home.

Outside of their home Rico, Derrick, and Dante are playing in the pool. Linda is lying in her hammock reading a magazine. Travis is reading a book, Art of War by Sun Tzu. Derrick notices a light reflecting from the scope out of the hills but continues to play in the pool. Mercandel is a few feet away seasoning meat for the grill.

Combs sweats uncontrollably watching the officer take aim. He can see Mercandel through the kitchen window by the sink and then looks at Combs, "Sir, are you going to serve Mercandel his warrant? He's in clear view."

Detective Combs still watching closely, "I am." From a distance Rodrigo is watching from his SUV. He sees Detective Combs walking toward the Mercandel house to serve the warrant.

A strong gust of wind blows Linda off balance in her hammock. Travis turns around immediately. In the process he sees a red dot light hit the edge of the window, quickly disappearing. He looks harder to make sure. Linda chuckles underneath her breath, "Derrick! Come help me up." Derrick walks over to help her.

Rico calls out, "Father...?"

Linda stands up, Travis' seriousness gets her attention. "Travis?"

Mercandel is standing washing a couple of dishes in the kitchen when he sees Combs walking down his driveway from the kitchen window, gun ready. He stops preparing the meat and wipes his hands on his apron going to meet Combs at the door.

Combs stops in front of a group of trees that is near the front of the house where he can't be seen by the other cops. Mercandel walks out of the kitchen into the hallway about to head toward the front door when he sees Travis. Travis looks terrified at Mercandel, mutters, "Father...." He turns and walks toward his son.

Mercandel looks with a blank face, "I know." Mercandel's entire facial expression changes as he moves closer to his son. Combs is still at the front door, he takes a deep breath, then FIRES THREE SHOTS in the air. He yells into his radio... "Shots fired, shots fired!"

Behind the house the second Officer sees Combs running from the front of the house. The first Officer shoots Travis through the back patio glass door. The glass door SHATTERS.

Mercandel stops in his tracks. The bullet hits Travis in the back and exits through his chest. He falls forward further into the house. Linda runs toward her son. Linda is screaming frantically, "Travis!" Gunfire and sparks of light come from the direction of the hills. Rico, Derrick, Dante, and Linda are shot down in cold blood. Mercandel breaks down at the sight of his slaughtered family.

He takes Travis in his arms. Travis goes in and out of consciousness. He gurgles on his own blood and struggles to breathe with tears sliding down his face looking at Mercandel. In the distance Sirens can be heard as ambulances race to the house along with the chatter of police officers.

Mercandel weeps. "Shh, shh, son. Help is on the way. Just hold on for your father." He rocks Travis back and forth. "I'm sorry. I'm so sorry." His head falls lifelessly to the side. Mercandel begins to groan with fury, "they are all I had!!!!!!"

Rodrigo is sitting down in a black Mercedes Benz then he picks up his cell phone, it's done. Lopez is at home sitting on the couch, he hangs up the phone."

CHAPTER 8

At the boarding school in Africa Sky, now 11, dressed in tailored clothes, sits with her feet crossed. She is studying. Lifting her head, she stares out the window at the villagers feeding some elephants in the distance. After watching for a while, she returns to her studies.

When Mercandel walks in she looks up and sees him. She gives him a beautiful smile. He sits across from her as she closes her textbook.

Mercandel returns the smile then he gives her a hug. "Sky How's school coming?"

Sky returns his hug, "Hello Father." Sky, with a large smile, "It is well. Where are the boys? It feels like such a long time since I have seen everyone."

Mercandel looks off briefly then turns back and gives Sky his full attention, your studies are very important. You will need to stay focused."

Sky humbly, "Father, where are my brothers?"

Mercandel turns away sadly, then turns back to Sky, "It

will be a while before my next visit. In the meantime, we will converse every 1st Monday of the month at 7 pm. No excuses."

Sky confused, "Father, what has happened? Where are my brothers?"

Mercandel teary-eyed, "Sky, you are a strong and disciplined young lady. We will have to move forward from here."

Sky puts her head down and her eyes becomes teary, "Yes, Father."

"I came to bring you this." Mercandel pulls out the book, *Art of War*. There is faint blood splattered on the edge of the pages. "Read it. We will discuss it the next time we talk."

Sky looks at the book closely, "this is Dante's favorite book."

Mercandel stands and Sky stands as well. They hug and he begins to walk away. Sky screams "Father!!!" Mercandel stops. "Where are my brothers?"

Turning slightly in her direction, looking at the ground, he whispers, "They were killed."

Mercandel picks his head up and walks out. She opens the cover of the book and inside are the pictures taken of the Mercandel family. She begins to SOB.

CHAPTER 9

Two years later at Harvard University in the Office of Careers, Mercandel is sitting at his desk reading a book by Malcolm X. Diem Lee, a Korean male student in his mid 20s, knocks on the door. Lee walks into his office and stands in front of Mercandel's desk. Mercandel never looks up.

Lee, standing there, hands in his pockets, "Professor?"

Mercandel leans back in his chair never looking up, "I'd rather you change your tone. It needs to be orchestrated to the greatest point, especially when you are speaking to a man that can change your life forever." Mercandel then looks up at Lee, "Mr. Lee, can you tell me your meaning of success?"

Lee eager to speak, "Success is surviving the odds of young men in my country."

Mercandel leans forward. "So, you are telling me, Mr. Lee, that you are successful because you left your country?"

Lee trying to explain himself, "I'm saying I got out on the strength I have. It was either them or me. But I'm a changed man now. Too bad somebody else had to pay for it. But that's life."

Mercandel laughs and removes his glasses and places them on top of the book. He leans back in his chair to give Lee his full attention. Mercandel totally nonchalant, "Excuse me, what were you saying?"

Lee pauses, "You didn't hear what I just said?"

Mercandel looking confused, "Well Mr. Lee, I was listening to you until you got to the part..." He pauses. "Of either 'them or me' and son quite frankly, I don't waste time. So, I tuned out everything else after that sentence."

Lee raised his tone and is becoming upset; "the most important thing is that I made it over here."

Mercandel looking around, "Here!...America!" Mercandel burst into a laugh..."the land of the free, the big apple. Well in case no one hasn't told you, I welcome you to Babylon. Check it out in the Bible Revelation 16:19. I understand we are here for a brief moment, all wrong will and shall be judged. So shall a man reap, so shall he sow." Mercandel shakes his head as Lee is looking on in awe. "I mean it's a hell of a situation." Mercandel paused for a moment..."You are not here because you were the nicest kid on the block who earned his way faithfully. That's what really matters." Mercandel rises, comes from behind his desk and stands in front of Lee, "A real man has an explanation for every corner of his life."

Mercandel shakes his head and gazes around the room. "Business is another definition for problem. We all have problems. The question is, how do you deal with yours?"

Lee looks at Mercandel. Mercandel points his left index finger at the palm of his right hand. "The conscience has to be in control and directed. If you can't sleep at night because of guilt, you're not controlling your conscience. It's controlling you."

Lee sits in the nearby chair. Lee sarcastically, "So, what do you suggest I do about my conscience Professor?"

Mercandel makes it back to his chair. "I'm glad I have your full attention now. Out of respect, I wanted to hear what you had to say, but you started talking bullshit... and You know I don't have time for that."

Lee looks with a silly smirk, "Bullshit."

Mercandel nods his head towards Lee, "No matter what you have done in your past, I shouldn't be able to bring up an incident that would move one emotion inside of you without you wanting it to move. No man should have that much power over your emotions."

Lee confused," Sir, is that why you requested my presence? So we can talk about ill feelings and the conscience."

Mercandel laughs, "I like that! Besides, frankly it's your father's fault. He was the one that messed you up." Mercandel stares into Lee's eyes. Lee bursts into laughter. Mercandel grins, then Mercandel gives a direct look with a half of smirk on his face. "What's so fucking funny?"

Lee became very serious, "He thought he could break me...he almost did though. He almost did."

Mercandel becomes serious and stares at Lee for a brief moment, "It's the heart and mind that haven't healed. We should do some healing, it's good for the soul."

Lee becomes very emotional, "A five-year old kid walking around with a broken arm was his way of making a man out of me."

Mercandel with a stern look on his face, responds, "Okay!"

Lee totally confused, "Okay??"

Mercandel picks his pen off the desk and he points it at Lee, "See the bullets you used, should have been used on your father. We're going to leave this weekend to go to Korea. You would have had an easier sentence because of what?"

Lee calms down. "I would have had an explanation. So Mercandel, why are we going to Korea? "

Mercandel smiles. "Don't you want to be free? I'm

going to walk you through the healing process." Lee stands up.

Mercandel grabs his book and puts on his glasses. He walks toward the door, "Unless they are willing to give their life for yours, one man should never have that much power over you. I know that must really piss you off when you think about it. Get a good night's sleep, I will pick you up at 0900." Mercandel said bluntly, "Sharp!"

Mercandel opens the door for Lee who walks out and Mercandel turns off the light, closes and locks the door behind him with a key.

◆ ◆ ◆

Mercandel is sitting on a bench on one of the Patios at Harvard University. His eyes squinted as peers towards the sun. Nathan D'Angelo is a well- built black man standing 6'2" tall in his mid 20s. He moseys toward Mercandel hugging a woman.

Before Nathan is able to speak a word, Mercandel yells making eye contact with Nathan, "In my school's attendance, there are exactly two-thousand five-hundred and thirty-nine students and one-hundred and two dropouts." Therefore, I know there is only ONE Nathan D'Angelo." The woman gives Mercandel an awful stare and walks pass him slowly rolling her eyes.

Nathan becomes upset, "Say bro, that wasn't cool, embarrassing me like that."

Mercandel squints his eyes looking at Nathan "You embarrassed yourself son when you couldn't follow simple directions."

Nathan boldly, "You never said I couldn't come with someone!"

Mercandel looks off, "And I never said you could! You are taught in kindergarten to ask if you don't know."

Nathan grinding his teeth, "Man look-a-here!"

Mercandel looks at Nathan then he looks around and then back at Nathan, "Who do you really think you are Mr. D'Angelo? Chasing behind another man's na-na landed you 3 years in juvi for your so-called lil' boo who flipped the switch on you and said you raped her."

Mercandel gives Nathan a half-cocked smile and nodded his head at him, "The front page huh?"

Nathan is speechless. He sits on the bench next to Mercandel never taking his eyes off of him. Nathan pause for a moment then he looks at Mercandel, "How do you know that bro?"

Mercandel responds, "First, answer my question. Why are you still stupid? Son, if you feel a woman is acting in a manner you wouldn't want your sister or mother to act, then tell her how to act." Mercandel raises his voice and laughs. "Remember this, if you speak to the whore in her, the whore will answer. But, if you speak to the queen within her, the queen will answer."

Nathan looks around at all the other students and pretty girls passing and points his arm out at them. "Man, I don't give a damn about none of these females out here."

Mercandel begins to look around also in amazement. Then he turns back and gives Nathan his full attention. "How long are you going to continue to play with fire before you learn? Instead of hurting all these women behind one woman, you should just handle the one you have a problem with. That's resentment. I really do understand. But, you won't truly live until your problem goes away." She has taken something from you that will never be replaced...Time."

Mercandel straightens his tie. Nathan LAUGHS underneath his breath, "Man, you are so funny. You clowning me, huh?" Nathan looks around. "Who's punking you? We not living T.V, we are living real life out here."

Mercandel looks around. "Do you see cameras out here and a producer saying lights, camera, action?" He pauses, "of course you don't. This weekend I'm going to be a little busy with another student. So, next weekend will be perfect. We will fly to Las Vegas and give Mrs. Cynthia a little visit." Mercandel looks at Nathan.

Nathan with a surprise look on his face, "Cynthia!?!

Mercandel nodded, "Yes. You sold drugs and you did kill, but it was all about your respect. The system does it every day. But for her to turn on you and say you raped her-NO! We are not having that!"

Nathan responds, "Man, whatcha talking about we?" I didn't see your ass in the courtroom when they were trying to railroad my ass."

Mercandel smirks, "But I'm here now." Mercandel walks off and leaves Nathan on the bench. "If she did that to one of my sons, that same day she would have been history." Nathan stands motionless staring at Mercandel as he walks off.

◆ ◆ ◆

Mercandel sits at a table reading a book at Harvard University in the Library. As the last student walks out, a slender homely-looking Hispanic male in his mid 20s named Antonio Sanchez strolls in. He notices that there is no one in there besides Mercandel. He strolls over to the table and takes a seat directly in front of Mercandel. Mercandel reads for the next couple of minutes. Mercandel smiles, "Now that's imperative." He continues to read.

Antonio clears his throat, "Hello...Hello?"

Mercandel looks up. "Oh Hello." Mercandel continues to read.

Antonio getting a little agitated, "How long do I need to sit here before you acknowledge my presence?"

Mercandel puts his book down on the table and stares at Antonio. Mercandel looks at Antonio straight in his eyes, "I requested that you be here at 10:00." Mercandel glances at his WATCH. "It is 10:00...now."

Antonio laughs. "Maybe I needed to come early because I have a class at 10:30. Besides, isn't this just some counseling meeting?"

Mercandel responds, "This will be by far the most important meeting of your life, more than judgment day itself. So, etch this memory deep, deep down into your skull."

Antonio responds, "Deep down in my skull?"

Mercandel points at his head with one of his fingers with a straight look, "Deep. Down. In. Your. Skull. Son, do you believe in the old saying, "The early bird gets the worm?"

Antonio responds, "On my block, we do!"

Mercandel winks at Antonio, "But you left your block for a reason. Why leave something behind if you're going to sit and fiend for it?"

Antonio leans forward towards Mercandel. "Because I love money!"

Mercandel rubs both his hands together, "I know you do, every man does. You did time behind it too." Antonio sits back slowly. Mercandel curiously ask, "Accountant? I'm glad I persuaded you to major in something to earn yours faithfully upon character." Mercandel moves closer to Antonio, "Who in the hell did you think was going to hire you with a felony for stealing credit card numbers?"

Antonio looks around to make sure no other students was nearby, "You don't understand Sir. I owe this dude big time! Sixty-thousand dollars."

Mercandel looks at Antonio unconcerned. "Always pay your debtors off. That will clear your conscience as a man, but always have a plan B. Most importantly, never be afraid to die. Because most likely if you don't pay up they going to kill your ass."

Antonio leans towards Mercandel, "What you fail to realize my friend, Man, all that shit is in the past."

Mercandel leans closer to Antonio and whispers, "Pay what you owe."

Antonio raises his tone just a little, "Where am I going to get sixty thousand dollars from? What, you want me to go rob a bank!?!"

Mercandel straightens his composure and fixed his tie. "Why are you having an attitude with me? That's your monkey on your back! So, out of curiosity, how are you planning on paying him his money back?"

Antonio puts his hands in the pockets of his pants, "I don't know, Sir."

Mercandel standing looking Antonio straight in his eyes

with a slight smirk, "I guess at the time, being locked up was the best thing that could have happened to you."

Antonio looks away for a brief moment. "I'm not planning on going back."

Mercandel steps back, "I understand; truly I do, you did what you had to do for your mother and your siblings to survive. Nonetheless, never leave a debt behind, either pay him or kill him! It's simple. Pay him or kill him. But only in that order, pay him if you have to rob a bank to do it. Dignity son!"

Antonio glances around, No matter how you are looking at it, "I'm dead meat."

Mercandel points at Antonio then himself and Antonio eyes gets big confused, "You and I are going to handle that." Mercandel nodded his head with a smirk.

Antonio beginning to get loud, "Are you crazy? Naah, naah bro, this cat here is no joke."

Mercandel's entire facial expression changes, became extremely serious, "A joke for who? I'm no joke son. The third weekend of this month, we're going back to the Bronx, New York."

Antonio pauses, "For what?"

Mercandel grins, "Let someone stand up for you at least once in your life."

Antonio starts laughing uncontrollably, "You're funny! For a minute, I thought you were serious."

Mercandel stands up and stretches. He walks off without looking back, "For the record... I am serious." Mercandel exits the library while Antonio sits at the table watching him until the GLASS DOORS CLOSE behind him.

◆ ◆ ◆

Mercandel walks into the Chemistry class in the Science lab at Harvard University and then sits at the teacher's desk while Timothy McGee, a Caucasian Country Boy in his mid 20s, is mixing chemicals together for a project. Timothy glances around and notices Mercandel but continues to work on his project.

Moments later, Timothy removes his goggles and gloves. He walks over to Mercandel. Timothy looks at Mercandel, "I would like to apologize, Sir, for not meeting with you. I had a very important project to complete."

Mercandel responds with a smile, "Thank you." Pauses, then states, "The meeting wasn't a part of your academics. It's impressive that you're self-motivated to discover something the next man hasn't yet. That's what makes a great man."

Timothy gestures with his head, "I always like to be a step ahead."

Mercandel begins to clap, "I wouldn't have survived without being a step ahead. I slipped once, and that was my last time."

Timothy McGee turns a chair around and sits in it backwards next to Mercandel, "I personally like to educate myself in my spare time. An idle mind is a devil's workshop."

Mercandel responds, "So I've heard." Mercandel looks at him with a small sideways grin,

"Turn your chair around so you can look me in my eyes. Always give another man full eye contact and sit correctly in your seat. Slouching is insufficient for a man."

Timothy McGee stares at Mercandel, gets up from his chair. He moves to the chair in front of Mercandel and takes a seat, "Now you have my full attention, Sir!"

Mercandel with a blank look says, "Thank you." He continues, "Make sure you do not miss any mixed emotions or expressions. Anyone can speak out of their mouths, but the expression tells on the conscience and exploits a man's soul. Never take for granted what another man says, but always look for motives and you will begin to find it in a man's expression."

Timothy smiles and looks off for a moment, then turns back and faces Mercandel. Timothy, "You don't sound like you should be a counselor."

Mercandel leans in closer to Timothy. Mercandel leans closer to give deeper eye contact, "What do you see in my eyes?" Timothy pauses and stares into Mercandel eyes, then he breaks eye contact. Mercandel never breaks eye contact. Timothy is so nervous, he fidgets with his hand, "I see strength, dignity, pain, resurrection!"

Mercandel smiles, "Do you see death?"

Timothy facial expression changes "I wasn't looking that hard, Sir."

Mercandel responds, "If I was coming in here to kill you, would you want to know?"

Timothy begins to look uncomfortable, "Why would you want to kill me?"

Nonchalantly, Mercandel responds, pausing, "Maybe because...I just want to." Then he looks up at the ceiling. "Let me see what my motive will be..." Mercandel smiles. "Because I just want to."

Timothy with uncertainty, "I guess that would be sufficient enough if that's your reason."

Mercandel smiles. "You are correct! If a man has a nine-millimeter handgun pointed at your head about to blow it off, does it matter the reason? His reason may not be sufficient enough for you, but he's still going to blow your fucking head off."

Timothy responds, "I wish my father was more like you."

Mercandel looks with a smirk, "Your father could never be like me. Your mother, Mrs. Gloria, you shouldn't be angry with her, she's helpless." He laughs.

Timothy looks off. Timothy becomes curious, "How do you know about my family?"

Mercandel says "What family? The ones that gave birth to you? Nothing personal, I did an extensive background check, comprende?"

Timothy looking at Mercandel, "That sounds legitimate now that you put it that way. I would like to see my mother though...I kinda think of her every now and then."

Mercandel points at Timothy's chest, "When you love someone, you think about them all the time. Anyone that is not in your heart shouldn't be thought about at all. It's pointless!"

Timothy becomes sadden, "She never really stood up for me as her son."

Mercandel paying close attention to Timothy's emotions, "Give her a break! She cannot and will not stand up for herself. Do you think he should be dead?"

Timothy responds, "You know; he'll probably be better off if he were dead. It's just too bad I don't want his blood on my hands."

Mercandel laughs, "Do you really mean that? Come on, you've got to be kidding." Mercandel stares at Timothy as they both begin to laugh. He stands up and glances around the lab. "I'm glad you like it here as your safe haven. Danger and knowledge brings power and respect. No one wants to piss off a dangerous man."

Mercandel gets up and his body is angled towards the

door, "I'm going to get back with you on that." Mercandel exits the room.

CHAPTER 10

It's night time in Korea, Mercandel and Lee drive up to a bar in a small town. They park and sit there. Lee looks at Mercandel, "How long are we going to sit here?"

Mercandel never looks at Lee, "As long as it takes." Lee's voice cracks, "Someone might notice the car just sitting here."

Mercandel tells Lee, "Well scoot down."

Lee adjusts in the seat and says "I'm not scared, just don't want to be caught."

Mercandel still watching, "I didn't ask you anything! Being scared is not the problem. Scared ass people kill people every day. The question is can you get away?"

Mercandel pulls out a drink and two sandwiches. He hands one to Lee. Mercandel begins to eat as Lee watches anxiously for his father. "Lee, please let me know when you see your father."

Lee looks at Mercandel strangely, "Do you do this kind of thing all the time? How do you sleep at night knowing that there may be repercussions?"

Mercandel smirks, "I stopped sleeping a long, long time ago."

Lee glances across the street, then turns back around and looks closer. A party of four exit the restaurant strolling and chatting. Startled by the sight, Lee whispers as he points at a man. "That's him right there, that's him. With the blue shirt on."

Mercandel walks across the street. He stands along the building, waiting for Mr. Lee. He then walks toward Mr. Lee. Mercandel and Mr. Lee meet, Mercandel elbows him in the nose. Mr. Lee grabs his face in pain. Mercandel grabs Mr. Lee by his jacket and jerks him into a nearby alley causing him to fall to the ground; then Mercandel slams his head on the cement three times.

Mercandel, "Don't you ever in your life put your hands on another child."

Mercandel raises Mr. Lee's head up, then bangs it again on the cement.

Mr, Lee, in agony, pleads "Let me go please. I'm sorry. I promise."

Mercandel hits Mr. Lee head on the cement yet again, "I said don't you ever raise a finger or your voice at another child again in your life. Because if I find out, I'm going to bring you back to this same alley and beat your head in until your brains come pouring out."

Mr. Lee bleeding from his head and nose falls unconscious onto the ground. Mercandel walks out of the alley and strolls over to the car and hops in and starts the car.

"I think he will remember our little conversation for the rest of his life." Lee stares at him for a moment. Mercandel returns the gaze. Mercandel sits still in the car for a moment, then turns to Lee "Don't let anything or anyone, try to take your peace of mind because at the end of the day, a peaceful mind is priceless."

Lee responds "Yes Sir."

♦ ♦ ♦

Mercandel is back in the United States sitting in a coffee shop waiting for Nathan to appear. Sipping a cup of hot tea, he spies Nathan as he enters the coffee shop. Nathan gives Mercandel eye contact all the way until he takes his seat.

Mercandel still sipping "You know that's how your girl got you the first time, being late on your game plan."

Nathan smirks, "You waited for me because you knew I was coming."

Mercandel responds, "I waited for you because I'm tired of you falling behind." Mercandel rises and walks off.

Nathan lingers behind staring at him. Nathan running after Mercandel trying to explain himself, "I mean like, what are you going to do exactly? Do you know where she is?"

Mercandel with a sudden zest of energy, "Of course!"

Nathan concerned, "What's the backup plan?"

Mercandel smirks, "We will figure it out once we get there.

Nathan stops in his tracks, "So, you're about to do whatever you do without a backup plan?"

Mercandel comes to an abrupt stop with his back turned to Nathan. Mercandel turns to Nathan, "You are the backup plan!"

Nathan becomes upset, "You know that's some bull, right? I'm just a freshman in college."

Mercandel continues to stroll out the coffee shop. Astonished, Nathan just stands there; then he follows Mercandel.

◆ ◆ ◆

Mercandel and Nathan drive slowly past the strip club in Las Vegas. He drives one more block and stops. While inside the car Mercandel scans the scene.

Nathan stares at him, "So, why are we stopping a block from the joint?"

Mercandel still scanning the scene, "You're going to get down in the back seat until I say to get up. Before you cross over, I am going to need your shirt."

Nathan, shocked, "My shirt?"

Mercandel looks at him then back to scanning the scene, "Did I stutter?"

Nathan takes off his shirt and hands it to Mercandel. Nathan still confused, "Why do you want my shirt?"

Mercandel still scanning the scene, "You ask too many questions. Now get in the backseat."

Nathan crossed into the backseat and gets down immediately. Mercandel tears off three long pieces from the shirt and sticks it in his pocket and throws the rest in the backseat with Nathan. Nathan sees a silver nine millimeter gun in the glove compartment and watches Mercandel put it in the back of his pants as he gets out of the car.

Nathan becomes a little uneasy, "What's the gun for?"

Mercandel smiles at Nathan with a half-cocked grin, "In case some physical negotiation is needed." Nathan watches Mercandel adjust his shirt to cover the gun and then heads to the strip club.

While Mercandel is standing outside of the strip club he notices a street camera pointing in his direction. He opens the door to a blast of loud music and customers enjoying themselves.

His clean patent leather shoes stop at the entrance. Mercandel walks inside of the strip club and glances around keeping his head low. He notices Cynthia, a stripper in her late 20s, dancing on stage. He walks past the bar keeping a low profile. He walks up to the stage and shows Cynthia five one-hundred dollar bills. He reaches out for her hand and smiles at her. Cynthia looks up at the bouncers and nods her head while she gets off the stage and walks with Mercandel. They hold hands down the hall towards an Exit door.

Cynthia smiles, "You want me to take a walk with you for five hundred bucks?"

Mercandel smiles, Something like that."

Cynthia starts rubbing all over her body, "Where are we going..."

Mercandel responds, "We are going to take a slow walk down memory lane."

Cynthia stops in her tracks, "Through an exit door?"

Mercandel stops. "There is a storage room right before the exit door." He puts his hand over Cynthia's mouth as she tries to scream while he drags her into the storage room.

He flips the light switch on as he pushes Cynthia against the door. He takes out his gun as he slowly removes his hand warning her with his eyes not to say a word! Wide-eyed and trembling, she nods.

He points the gun at her head! She starts whimpering. Mercandel puts one of his fingers against his lips as he snaps, "Be quiet and take off your heels."

Cynthia is trembling as she takes off her stilettos and gives them to Mercandel. He grabs them. Mercandel pulls out one of Nathan's shirt strips and ties her hands together. He then uses another strip to tie over Cynthia's mouth to muffle her screams.

Mercandel raises his tone slightly, "The next time you decide to walk in a courtroom to lie on someone..." Mercandel stabs Cynthia in both her knees with the stiletto. Cynthia falls unto the floor as muffled screams and whimpering come from her.

Mercandel in a humble voice, "Please think of the repercussions. Lies eventually catch up with you." Mercandel stands straight up looking down at Cynthia. Mercandel fixes his suit and uses the third strip to wipe his hands and her shoes and doorknob to remove his prints.

Mercandel looks down at her, "You may want to look into a career change; I don't think you will be getting on a pole anytime soon." He then exits the storage room and walks out of the club.

Mercandel gets inside the car and drives off. "You can get up now."

Nathan still shirtless climbs over the backseat to get back in the front, "You should have told me my $75 shirt was a part of the plan."

Mercandel looking forward "I did. I said, you were my back-up plan."

Mercandel smirks at Nathan and chuckles, "There's a jacket on the backseat that you can use."

Nathan reaches back, grabs the jacket and zips it up. "Did you really walk in there and shoot her?"

Mercandel smiles, "Bullets are not free! You can always improvise."

Nathan stares at Mercandel for a moment "So, what's next?"

Nathan peers out the side view mirror to see if anyone is following them. Mercandel responds, "School."

Nathan still looking out the window, "Why did you bring me with you? I know there's a motive for everything."

Mercandel smirks. "Nathan, you came because you wanted to be here to make sure the job got done. Besides, what would be my motive without you?"

Nathan suddenly becomes quiet in disbelief. Timidly, he asks "Are you serious?"

Mercandel responds, "If I go down, you go down. But remember one thing son, I always land on my feet. Loyalty is priceless, remember that son. I may fall, but I promise I will always land on my feet."

Nathan turns around and continue to look out the window, "School tomorrow I guess?"

Mercandel smiles and wink his eye, "Don't be late."

◆ ◆ ◆

Antonio is waiting in the New York airport, until ten o'clock strikes. He rises and strolls outside. Mercandel arrives in a rental car. He picks Antonio up at ten o'clock on the dot. Antonio gets into the car, "Damn bro! I thought something went wrong."

Mercandel responds, "How come? It's ten o'clock."

Antonio responds with a slight attitude, "Yeah, I understand that, but sometimes shit happens."

Mercandel direct, "Not in my book!"

Antonio looking around, "Sir, we're not going to use this same car, are we?"

Mercandel never looking at him, "No, we're going to steal a car to handle our business."

Antonio inquisitive, "So where are we going to get this other car from? I'm on probation and I have only a month and two days to go. I cannot leave my fingerprints, D.N.A., hair follicles on nothing!"

Mercandel creeps up a side street, "Son, you worry too much." Mercandel and Antonio drive up to an old car.

Antonio, "So what now?"

Mercandel looks slightly at Antonio, "You just watch and observe, you talk too much."

Mercandel pointing at the clock on the dashboard, responds, "You drive exactly six blocks down making sure no one notices you. Park, get out, eat something and start walking down the street. Keep that hood on. I will come and find you".

Antonio snaps, "ARE YOU CRAZY!?! I can't be walking around here like it's all good."

Mercandel looks at him and then calmly gets out the car. Antonio drives off.

Mercandel strolls across the street to a car parked there. He pops the lock in a matter of seconds. Mercandel gets in the car, hot wires it and drives down a couple of blocks searching for Antonio. He finds him pacing back and forth. Mercandel blows his horn and Antonio scurries over and hops into the car holding a sandwich.

Antonio is nervous and breathing hard!! Mercandel looks at him, "What's wrong with you?"

Antonio is holding his chest, "You told me not to ask any more questions."

Mercandel, "Now I'm asking you a question.

Antonio pauses, "Professor, what in the hell took you so damn long?"

Mercandel smirks, "Perfection."

Mercandel and Antonio drive up to a bar in the Bronx, Antonio sits in the passenger seat quiet. "Is there a problem son?"

Antonio responds "I want him to see my face. Well I'm glad that you have the balls to stand up, but don't pick my time to do it."

Antonio asserts, "I need to stand up to him as a man to negotiate how I can pay off my debt."

Mercandel looks around and smiles, "Alright then, go right ahead!" Mercandel jumps out the car holding a briefcase and Antonio follows. Mercandel walking at a steady pace, "Now remember, it's about having heart." Mercandel trails behind Antonio with one of his hands covering the nine millimeter gun with his shirt and the briefcase in his other hand.

Antonio walks into the bar first with Mercandel a few feet behind him. He lingers around with his arms behind his back. Gochaux, the dealer, is a Spanish man in his mid 40s. Gochaux and three others are drinking and playing cards. As Antonio approaches the table. Gochaux notices him and laughs, "Oh, Antonio. Look at my son y'all!"

Mercandel stands at the bar watching the T.V. with one of his hands behind his back holding the briefcase. Antonio looks at Gochaux, "Well Sir, I'm here to tell you that I managed to get my life under control. I have a full scholarship to Harvard University."

Gochaux looks at Antonio, "Where is my money?"

Mercandel steadily watches from the corner of his eyes. Antonio, "I came to you like a man."

Gochaux upset, "Well, you will leave in a body bag. Where's my fucking money?"

Antonio is getting upset, "I'm trying to negotiate with you."

Gochaux throws his glass of wine at Antonio; but misses him, "How about this for a negotiation? If I don't get my money in twenty-four hours, I'm going to kill your mom and your sister."

Mercandel walks to the table, puts his briefcase down and opens it. It's full of money. Gochaux looks at it.

Mercandel smiles, "That's your money to the very last penny."

Gochaux, "This is between me and Antonio. Who are you?"

Mercandel responds, "You don't want to know who I am."

Gochaux stares at Mercandel for a moment. Gochaux curious "What about interest?"

Mercandel glances at one of the men, "Do you have insurance?

"Yea, I have insurance." Mercandel pulls out his gun and shoots the man. He looks at Gochaux, "Your interest." Mercandel looks at everyone at the table, "Is there any other issues we need to address?"

Gochaux is staring at the fallen man; then turns and glares at Mercandel. Gochaux gives Mercandel a harsh look, "No, there is no problem, not at all."

As Antonio and Mercandel turn and proceed to stroll out of the bar. Gochaux grabs for the gun on the fallen man's hip. He looks up to see Mercandel watching through a mirror in the bar. Mercandel staring through the window as he walks away, "You don't want to do that."

Gochaux slowly puts his hand down and maintains eye contact with Mercandel until Antonio and Mercandel walk out and then jump into the car.

Inside of the car Antonio doesn't say a word. Mercandel drives off slowly and then turns to face him. Mercandel, "No matter what someone does for you, everyone has a motive! It boils down to the game. Are you down for me like I'm down for you? Are you willing to kill for me if I kill for you?"

They exchanged cars and dropped the stolen car in a rough neighborhood running with the windows rolled down.

◆ ◆ ◆

Mercandel drives up to Timothy's parents' beautiful Mansion home. Timothy sits in the car staring into the open fields. Timothy, "I really appreciate you coming here with me to face both of them."

Mercandel, "Well, if you feel talking to your father will clear your conscience, then that's fine with me." Mercandel snaps the clip into his gun. He puts his head down for a moment.

Timothy takes a sip of water from his water bottle, "What are you doing?"

Mercandel looks through the rear-view mirror checking his appearance. Then he closes his eyes and puts his head down for a brief moment. "I'm taking a moment of silence to pray that your father's attitude is pleasant today."

Mercandel raises his head up, opens the door and gets out. Timothy gets out the passenger side. They both walk up to the house. Timothy takes a deep breath, "I'm ready!" Then Timothy takes another DEEP BREATH.

Mercandel looks at Timothy, "No need to feel compelled to reconcile with your father. He is just a man."

Timothy grins at Mercandel. "You know what Professor? The worst thing a father could do to his son is not abuse, it's to pretend he doesn't exist. So, frankly I'm about to walk in here with a clear head with all options open."

Mercandel, "That's a good thing."

Timothy has his KEYS in hand and begins to unlock the door. Mr. and Mrs. McGee are sitting at the breakfast table. Mr. McGee is in a wheelchair. Timothy and

Mercandel approach the kitchen. Smiling happily, Mrs. McGee walks over and hugs Timothy. "Hello my Timothy!" Mrs. McGee gives Timothy a kiss.

Mr. McGee turns around and looks at Mercandel up and down. Mr. McGee turns and looks at Mrs. McGee, "I thought I told you to send Benny over here to change the locks."

Then he turns to Mercandel, "Who in the hell are you?"

Mercandel points to himself looking confused, "Are you talking to me?"

Mr. McGee returns the gesture with an attitude, "Yeah, you!"

Mercandel nods his head to Mr. McGee, "Oh, I'm not your problem." Mercandel pauses for a moment, "At least not yet."

Timothy walks towards the table, "Father, I came here today to speak to you one on one."

Mrs. McGee begins to look nervous as she wipes her mouth with a napkin, "Timothy, you know how busy your father is. Why didn't you call before you came?"

Mercandel turns his head. Mr. McGee sits back in his chair staring at Timothy. "That boy is not worth the air he breathes."

Mercandel looking down whispers something underneath his breath. Mercandel tapping his foot puts his hands behind his back. Mr. McGee turns all his attention back to Mercandel, "Back to you. What in the hell are you doing in my damn house with this waste of life?"

Mercandel looks up for a moment. He walks over to the back of Mr. McGee's chair and starts pulling him from behind.

Mercandel looks at Timothy and Mrs. McGee, "When you get tired of hearing his mouth, take him to the roof."

Mr. McGee yells, "Let me go you son of a bitch! Let my chair go."

Mercandel pulls Mr. McGee up a flight of stairs. He finds a room with a window and opens it and leans Mr. McGee over while he holds onto his chair.

Mercandel steadily slapping Mr. McGee on the side of his head, "From now on, you need to talk to your son and your wife with more respect as if you love them. Even if you have to pretend, because next time, I won't be pretending to drop your sorry ass out this window to the first floor."

Mr. McGee trembling and sweating, "Yes sir, no problem starting today right now."

Mercandel walks downstairs. Mrs. McGee is weeping. Timothy sits next to her and softly comforts her. Timothy looks at Mercandel, "What happened?"

"We had a man's heart to heart talk." as Mercandel

turns around nonchalantly and proceeds out of the front door.

CHAPTER 11

Mercandel is sitting in a chair reading a book in the library at his house. There is a digital clock next to him that reads 6:59. As he waits for Sky's call, he remembers his last visit:

He's outside in an open clear field sitting down quietly watching Sky,13, as she sits meditating with a Monk. Her feet are crossed as she listens to the Monk. They both get up after a few minutes than nod to each other standing still. Only seconds after they nod, Sky quickly runs and slides through the grass and picks up a bamboo stick on the ground. No sooner than she turns around the Monk is standing behind her and they begin to fight. Mercandel watches as he sees Sky's expertise in her skills have escalated. The Monk suddenly catches her in the face and knocks her to the ground. Mercandel eyebrow raises up as Sky falls and her nose is bleeding. She just lays there, not moving; tired

and hurting. The Monk says to her, "Get Up."
She raises her head still laying on her stomach
she screams angrily. NO! The Monk raises his
voice "Get Up Now!" she screams again with
tears in her eyes "NO!" Mercandel stands up
slowly. "GET UP NOW, OR YOU WILL DIE!"
Sky takes a deep breath as if thinking. Mer-
candel looks at the Monk and nods his head to
him. The Monk raises his feet over Sky's head
to stump it and she turns around suddenly and
grabs his foot with both hands and pushes him
back off of his feet with all her might and quickly
grabs the bamboo stick and cracks it instantly
across her leg and in a matter of seconds places
it under the Monk's throat. The Monk is frozen.
Sky is breathing hard, sweating uncontrollably,
and she's angry. Mercandel claps and then he
begins to walk off telling her, "It's just training.
You don't have to take it so personal".

The moment after the clock changes to 7:00 pm, his phone rings. Mercandel, underneath his breath, "Sky".

Sky, "Hello Father."

Mercandel smiles and puts down his book, "How's school?"

Sky, "School is well. Did you talk to the new guys you hired for your business?"

Mercandel picks up a pen and began tapping it on the

desk, "Yes. I think everything will work out. They are all very intelligent, young men."

Sky, "They have to be if you chose them."

Mercandel softly chuckles, "This is true. I will take them under my wing like I did you, they should be ready by the time they graduate."

Sky, "I have no doubts... Father, sometimes, I miss them."

Mercandel puts down his pen and leans back into his chair, "As do I, but we cannot live in the past. Rehashing their memory will not give them peace. We have to move forward. That is what they would have wanted."

Sky, "I know...Well, when will I come home and meet the new guys?"

Mercandel responds, "One day. When the time is right. But it won't be too long."

Sky, "Ok."

Mercandel closes his eyes in deep thought, "Goodnight Sky."

Sky, "Goodnight Father." Mercandel hangs up the phone.

CHAPTER 12

Five Years later in a Beverly hills restaurant Mercandel sips on a glass of White Zinfandel as he reads his Book. Lee, Nathan, Timothy, and Antonio are members of THE GLASS. They arrive at the same time approaching the table. Mercandel is observing a glass in his hands, "Well, good evening gentlemen. I'm sure you all have noticed your brothers. You will trust each other with your life and soul."

The Glass slowly begin to relax. Mercandel nods his head at each of them with a smile, "You can't break what can't be broken because you are fused. Which means, you all will think as one, consider as one, kill as one, and if needed, you will die for each other."

A waitress walks over to the table flirtatiously, "Excuse me, gentlemen, can I pour you a glass of wine?" None of the young men acknowledge her.

Nathan with a calm cool collected look, "The couple on the left side of the statue asked you for a glass of Merlot about eight minutes ago and they are still trying to get your attention. If we need you, we will call you."

As the waitress storms off, Mercandel clears his throat as he looks at each of them and smiles. He looks at the glass of water in front of him, "Glass is a hard, brittle substance, typically transparent or translucent made by fusing sand, soda, lime and other minerals. Gentlemen, you have the qualities of glass as each one of you fuse with each other making this evening, a night you will never forget."

Continuing, Mercandel said, "I would like to introduce each one of you to the other. Mr. Lee will be 'New York,' Mr. D'Angelo will be 'Cali,' Mr. Sanchez will be 'Detroit,' and Mr. McGee, 'Florida.' Florida is the chemist specializing in chemical weapons. Detroit will be your lawyer and you turn to him for any and all legal complications. New York will be the computer systems analyst for any and every aspect down to a computer chip that is smaller than a grain of rice and can grasp information from satellites. Cali is the accountant. He will have down to the penny of every man's account whether it's overseas, under the sea or floating on top of the sea."

The Glass glance at each other. Mercandel smiles as he looks deeply at each one of them, "So I have given you all the basic essentials that a businessman will need. I have been working with you all individually on special projects and it's time to bring them all together. There is no such thing as mistakes. This is what your lives mean to me, and these are the extremes you will go for each other. You are your brother's keeper."

CHAPTER 13

Mercandel walks into the police station in Beverly Hills as a mail carrier. He walks up to the officer sitting behind the desk. Mercandel kindly, "May, I use the phone? I need to call my supervisor."

The friendly Officer, "Sure, you can use the phone in Detective Barry's office. He's out for the day."

Mercandel smiles, "Thanks." Mercandel walks in the direction of the office. Moments later, Mercandel on the phone with a little notepad in his hand, "Thank you Mary. I am about to walk out of my office. How about you call me back with the confirmation number in about 30 minutes when it processes?" Mercandel responds, "Yes. Thank you so much. And if I change my mind, it will take 24 hours before it is put back on my policy, correct?" He tells Mary, "When you call back, I am at extension 562, Yes ma'am, Have a great day."

Mercandel hangs up the phone and walks out of the office. Combs is sitting down at his desk doing paperwork. The phone rings. He answers.

Mary, "Hello, this is Mary, from your insurance company. I am calling with your confirmation number."

Combs still looking through his paperwork, suddenly stops, confused, "Confirmation number? Confirmation number for what?"

Mary, "For the change in your policy we just spoke about earlier." Combs beginning to get irate, "Lady, I don't know who you are, but I did not talk to you and didn't change nothing on no policy."

Mary, "Ok sir. Is your name Mr. Donald Combs?"

Combs is confused, "Yes."

Mary, "What are the last four digits of your social?"

Combs responds with the info requested.

Mary, "Well, you changed your policy and removed fire protection on your house." Combs chuckles with disbelief, "I never talked to you to change a damn thing on my policy!!!"

Mary, "Sir, the change in your policy has been finalized and will take 24 hours to reprocess your account."

Combs stands up, "I have to wait 24 hours for you to fix a mistake that you made! I want to talk to someone who can fix this and compensate me for this bullshit."

Mary, "If you don't mind holding, I can get my supervisor for you."

Combs puts one of his hands on the top of his head in

aggravation, "Yeah, get your damn supervisor."

While Combs' is on hold, a fellow officer running over to his desk, yelling "Say Combs, your house is on fire!"

Combs turns around angrily, "What!?!"

"I said your house is burning down!"

Combs gets up immediately, drops the phone and runs out of the office. Speeding up to his home, Combs stops abruptly and jumps out the car. There are firemen putting out the fire. Neighbors stand outside looking. He runs up to the house hysterically. "What in the... it took me three years to build my house!" He looks around frantically, "Where are my dogs? Where are my dogs!?!" Moving frantically as he looks around the property, yelling, "Beauty, Beast, where are you?"

A fireman walks up to Combs, "Sir, we didn't find any dogs. Is there anyone with a key who could have gotten the dogs and accidentally started the fire in the house? Like a family member?"

Combs is panicking, "My dogs are my family." Combs grabs the fireman's jacket, "My dogs live in the house."

The fireman stated, "Someone must have gotten in and taken the dogs out before setting the fire. We did not find any dogs inside."

Another fireman walks over from the house, "Mr. Combs, did you have any fire insurance sir?" Combs looking lost, "The insurance company called and said I canceled it, but I didn't!"

The first fireman said, "I'm sorry to hear that sir. I'm sorry to hear that."

Combs, angry and dejected, walks back to his car and gets in. As he sits back exhausted, looking around carefully at the neighbors, Combs whispers "Mercandel."

Combs' phone rings. He picks it up answering, "What?"

The caller identifies himself. "This is Mark from your Insurance Company, I heard about your situation. Can you come into the office to get all of this straighten out?"

Combs dejectedly, "Yes."

Mark, said, "We have temporarily moved our office to the Main Branch bank while we are renovating."

Combs responds, "I'm on my way now."

Florida walks with two shepherd dogs on a leash in the park. He walks over to a woman sitting with a little girl, "Excuse me Ma'am, can you please watch my dogs for a couple of minutes while I go to the concession stand?"

The woman smiles, "Yes, I can. They are so beautiful. What are their names?"

Florida looks down at the dogs, "Samson and Delilah."

The Woman and the Little Girl play with the dogs as Florida walks off.

Combs arrives at the bank in record time. He enters the

bank lobby and looks around. He spots a well-dressed man and walks over to him. Combs addresses the gentleman stating, "I have an appointment with Mark from the insurance company."

The man turns his attention to Combs and smiles, "I am Mark." He shakes Combs' hand and guides Combs over to a nearby desk.

Cali acting as a manager is standing behind the Teller station as he watches Combs move over to the desk and then he leaves through a door to the back. As he is walking down the bank hallway, he is talking into his earpiece, he informs New York "Combs is here."

In a truck nearby, New York in front of a laptop typing, responds, "Okay, I'm on it." As he continues typing, He says "Let me know when you activate sound."

Cali sits down at the desk behind Combs. He grabs a small remote from inside the desk and activates the listening device that is already setup under the desk where Combs is sitting. Cali speaking quietly, "Activated."

New York sitting in the truck, "Perfect."

Detroit enters the truck moments later dressed in a hoodie and jeans. He states "There are seven cameras from the street that faces the bank and nearby areas."

New York not looking up says "Okay."

CHAPTER 14

Detective Rhonda, a Caucasian female in her mid 30s, walks into Lieutenant Watkins' Office with a file. She hands it to Watkins as he sits at his desk drinking a cup of coffee. Rhonda, "Good Morning Sir! This is the updated file you asked for."

Lieutenant Watkins shakes his head as he takes the file from Rhonda. He tells Rhonda that it has been 5 years since they have had Mercandel on their radar. He disappeared after his family was killed in the raid on his home.

Combs walks into the office, he looks at Rhonda sitting there. She looks back at him and cracks a smile. He says to Watkins, "Good Morning Sir." Combs turning to Rhonda asks, "How've you been girl? I haven't seen you in a while. Are you back to stay?"

Rhonda, "Yeah, I think so."

Combs goes and sits down in front of Watkins' desk. Watkins opens the file while Rhonda watches Combs carefully.

Watkins tapping the file, "This is the updated file on Dedrick Mercandel. You know he was working at Harvard and moved back here just recently."

Combs grimaced saying, "Lord, have mercy."

Rhonda asked, "Is there a problem? I read briefly into his file."

Combs said to Rhonda, "Before your time." Turning to Watkins in disbelief, "What the hell does he wanna come back here for? Is this dude like, dancing with death?"

Watkins, "That is just the problem, he moved back here. Why can't he go and be some other city's problem?" Turning his attention to Rhonda, "Thank you Rhonda."

Rhonda stated, "Mercandel relocated months later after the death of his family and worked at Harvard University as a Career Systems Analyst. I'm sure that after his family was killed, he just moved away." Rhonda continuing, "I really don't know any man who could deal with that and go on with his life like nothing ever happened. I just don't know about that, it's not registering well with me."

Watkins responded, "Dedrick Mercandel is not just any man." He noted, "I'm not quite sure if I will be underestimating his intelligence by calling him just a man."

Combs laughs and looks at Watkins, "This guy just can't be serious."

Lieutenant Watkins closed his eyes for a short moment, then opens them and looks out the window pensively, "What happened to his family was wrong. His sons were not criminals." Taking a breath, he said, "We were wrong. We took his family from him when we were supposed to take him from his family."

Rhonda utters, "Well, for what I have gathered, he hasn't had any trouble with the law, not even so much as a speeding ticket on his record. Every few years he gets charged, but the conviction never sticks. The drug lords had them a great candidate, smart, clever, always out of the spotlight, perfect family man and perfect kids. What more could you ask for?"

Watkins went on, "Mercandel went to private school his entire life. He was an only child. We even interviewed his teachers. All they had to say was that he was quiet and brilliant.

Combs, "He has no friends so there was no one to interrogate. Both parents and grandparents are dead. So, his family were his everything." Combs stated, "As far as I'm concerned, he's a dead man walking. I mean, he might have gone to Harvard to see how to make a nuclear bomb as far as we know." Combs adjusts and shifts in his seat.

Rhonda muses, "The only thing that really bothers me is the inner man. I'm sure this man has some type of fury or anger in his bones for what we've done. Revenge is probably living in him every day."

Watkins said, "Hopefully he learned his lesson."

Rhonda turns around, approaches the door, and stares back at Watkins. "With all due respect sir, we really never caught him. So therefore, did you complete the lesson?" Rhonda then walks out the door.

Combs clears his throat while looking at Watkins. Watkins points a finger at Combs. Combs responds, "Isn't this some shit! He knows you're watching him."

Lieutenant Watkins countered, "They are watching us!" And then stated, "They are not playing games."

Watkins then declared, "These four are way more dangerous than Mercandel could ever be because they have already been systematized. Mercandel took in all the information and filtered out all the bull shit and spoon fed them straight knowledge."

Watkins said to Combs, "I don't want any crap out of you. I'm putting you with Rhonda. She may be a rookie, but she's very smart and patient."

CHAPTER 15

At the Golf course in Beverly Hills Mercandel is playing golf alone and concentrating. Combs drives up in a golf-cart and stops inches from where Mercandel is standing. Mercandel never turning around.

Combs says, "It's a beautiful day today."

Mercandel responds casually, "Everyday a man can consciously inhale and exhale is a beautiful day. Why did you let Watkins talk you into taking this case? Why would you want to volunteer to lose your mind and your life all in one day?"

Combs, responds with a smile, "This is what the fuck I do. I catch bad ass boys like you." Nonchalantly, "Some of them I may kill. Depends on what mood I'm in that day."

Mercandel just hit a hole-in-one. Combs watching him begins clapping.

Mercandel turns around and looks at Combs. Then turns back to set up another shot." He tells Combs, "Give up the case."

Combs bursts into laughter. In a direct tone Combs responds, "My brother you got me fucked up."

Mercandel hits another hole-in-one. He turns around and points the golf club at Combs, with a smirk on his face and raises one eyebrow, "No my brother when you took this case THAT is when you fucked up."

Picking up his golf clubs, he heads back to the clubhouse leaving Combs standing in the middle of the fairway.

CHAPTER 16

In the hills of the firing range, there are targets of men, women, and children of different ethics. The targets are sliding back and forth. Mercandel is standing watching three young men as they practice. Antonio, Nathan and Timothy are laying on their stomachs with a Barrett M82 in each one of their hands. Diem Lee is standing besides Mercandel.

Mercandel lays out the list of rules and tips before they start shooting, "We don't kill children or women under any circumstances. You can wound them, but under NO CIRCUMSTANCES are any fatal injuries justified. The targets will come at you;" he bluntly states, "they are coming to KILL YOU. You must trust and rely on your own instincts and wits as well as trust your brother with your lives. Hit all targets in the heart. You each will take your turn and it comes down to just this. You have no other choice. You miss a shot one of you will be laying down in this field choking on your own blood. You know the paramedics are not going to get to you in time out here in the mountain."

Mercandel looks at his watch, "Lee you have exactly 3 minutes and 32 seconds to get around each target."

Mercandel looks at Lee who is looking at him with a sweat of nervousness. Mercandel tells Lee "God is real" then the timer BEEPS, Lee takes off running. The other Three begin shooting the targets. Mercandel stands there with his arms folded watching with his shades on.

CHAPTER 17

Detroit (Antonio) is sitting in a Beverly Hills restaurant working on his laptop. The restaurant owner, a man in his mid 60s is behind the bar cleaning glassware. The only other person there is the Security Guard standing just outside of the doors. As Detroit is focused on his laptop, the owner comments, "You all seem so much alike. Really my friend, life is not that serious."

Detroit sees the Security Guard walk away from his post through the window, shuts his laptop, and puts it into his briefcase. He gets up and exits the restaurant. The owner stares at Detroit as he walks past him. As Detroit is leaving, the owner states, "I didn't mean to make you feel uncomfortable buddy. But it's so quiet in here, you can hear a mouse piss on cotton."

Three gangsters walk up with a beer in their hand outside of the restaurant. One sits at the outside patio table in front of the restaurant. One is standing up watching the entire scene. The Security Guard walks on the side of the restaurant and meets up with the third one who asks, "What's up?"

The Security Guard nervously nods his head as he says, "He's in there. Make it quick."

The Gangster slides the Security Guard some money and then walks back toward the front of the restaurant to join the other two. Meanwhile the Security Guard walks in the opposite direction. When he meets up with the other two in front, he pulls a T-shirt from his back pocket and polishes Detroit's Lamborghini. As he is polishing the Lamborghini, he whispers, "You are coming home with me tonight."

He glances at the restaurant to see Detroit standing in the doorway with a briefcase in his hand. Detroit smirks. The gangster sitting at the table uttered, "This is a pretty bitch we got here. Whatcha think?" The other two laugh uncontrollably. "Say hommie, look at this handsome educated pretty boy!"

He tosses his beer on the ground. Beer bottle shatters while his partner walks over to Detroit and stands in his face pulling out a knife, "I'm gona take yo shit and you ain't going to do a mutherfucking thing about it."

Detroit glances at each of the men, "Today won't be a good day."

He grabs Detroit's shoulder and Detroit uses his briefcase to uppercut the gangster in the face. Then Detroit grabs his hand, spins, and breaks both of his arms. His partners run toward Detroit as he puts the briefcase down. Detroit grabs the nearest one and throws him through the glass of the restaurant.

Hearing the glass shatter, the restaurant owner looks up and sees a man flying through the front glass. He drops the glass he was holding and runs to the front door. Wide-eyed and scared, he sees Detroit take another man down using a Karate chop with one of his hands to the side of his neck. As blood shoots out the man's mouth, he sees Detroit kick the man's knee in as he falls to the ground.

Detroit looks around, walks to his briefcase, picks it up, walks to his car, and gets in. The gangster left standing yells, "This ain't over, I'm gonna see you again."

Detroit giving him a cold stare says "I don't think so." Detroit smiles coldly and drives off quickly. He makes it two blocks away, then presses a detonator and a large chemical explosion erupts inside of the restaurant. The destruction wreaks havoc for two blocks.

With sirens blaring, the police and EMTs arrive amid the chaos caused by the explosion. Outside of the restaurant, Policemen and EMTs are everywhere looking for survivors. People are screaming and running out of control in the streets. Watkins staring at the debris looks up as Combs walks over. "Lieutenant." Combs, pissed, says "You know this mess is going to be on CNN news."

CHAPTER 18

The Forensics Team has set up a tent nearby with all of their technology equipment. They sift through the debris and rubble hoping to understand exactly what happened and how it happened.

Rhonda leaving the Forensics tent walks over to Watkins. She removes the mask covering her mouth. Watkins states, "Whoever tried to kill whoever made sure they destroyed whatever else was around that breathed the same air."

Rhonda puzzled, asks, "Sir, what could have been the reason? There was only one gentleman that left prior to the bombing and a Security Guard whose body parts are across the street." Rhonda continues "Several other victims had prior criminal records in gang violence, but none of them would have had the knowledge and technology to actually make a chemical bomb. It was preset before the explosion as if a backup plan for a raw deal, maybe."

Watkins grimaced, "The street camera that was only

partially damaged was nearly three blocks away. It only showed an image of a man in a light-colored car."

Combs, "Whomever designed this chemical bomb knew what they were doing."

The Bomb Technician walks over to Watkins with a piece of metal in his hands. "Excuse me Sir, but we have a major problem here." Combs, Rhonda, and Watkins turn and give him their full attention. "Whoever designed this bomb had to be a chemist. Not just a chemist, but someone who constructed the exact amount of chemicals to explode and blow both power lines totally into shreds. They must have already known that the picture in the camera rolls its tape every twenty-four hours. The main tape recordings are on that corner...," pointing to the left, which holds tape recordings three days at a time before it is transferred to the 476th precinct."

Rhonda is confused. She looks at the post, then back at the bomb technician asking, "So what does that mean?"

The Technician answers, "That means you have an Einstein behind some deadly material that you shouldn't mess with. He calculates every inch, square foot, and millimeter to its precise point. Einstein left no room for error."

Watkins growls, "We will get to the bottom of this today!"

The Technician begins to walk off stating, "Somebody in this department better get to the bottom of this because if not, the F.B.I. will step in and they always make you guys look like helpless little babies."

Rhonda turns around and watches the Technician. She then turns back to Watkins, "You know Sir, the only way you became a good lieutenant is because you learned from the best of criminals."

Watkins upon reflection exclaims, "I hope Mercandel is not on the loose again. My God! Let it be anybody but him."

Rhonda morosely, "By far your greatest challenge is about to begin, because whoever he is, is much more clever than your everyday criminal." Rhonda walks off to her car leaving Watkins.

CHAPTER 19

In a Cabin in the deep woods of North Carolina Mercandel and The Glass are holding their monthly meeting. Florida (Timothy), Cali (Nathan), Detroit (Antonio), New York (Lee) all sit at the round table watching Mercandel as he prepares their favorite entrees in the kitchen. He walks into the dining area pushing a cart loaded with their meal. Mercandel places the food onto the table.

As he joins them asks, "May I lead grace?" The Glass bow their heads. "Thank you Almighty, the Alpha and the Omega. May my sons and I come together as one for the opportunities that you have blessed us with. By your grace alone we are here to honor your mercy as we bow our heads as a family." They all begin to eat quietly.

Detroit reporting states, "I searched the F.B.I. database inside out and they have classified it as a terrorist attack."

Mercandel responds, "Don't underestimate the mind of a man. The mind continues to think on."

Detroit, "Unfortunately, he took my word for granted."

Mercandel, "That's excellent, keep it business always, nothing personal."

New York adds, "Lieutenant Watkins has been searching the web for your whereabouts. Unfortunately, Combs is not too far behind. Every time they use their computer whether it's to tell the time, I have the name, location, and reference as if they are automatically exchanging information with me."

The Glass laughs. Mercandel "So I reckon they have a photographic memory of me."

Cali expounds, "He, them, their family, dog, grandmother or great grandmother will be pushing up daisies on my watch."

Mercandel suddenly looks at Cali upset, "Never that, never innocent people. Never ever children!"

Detroit, politely asks, "Sir, why is he targeting you?"

Mercandel states, "It's nothing personal son, he's just doing his job like we must continue to do ours." Mercandel laughs.

Cali looking confused, "That's funny sir?"

Mercandel quietly states, "Now you know what is so funny? It's how the police think they know everything. They believe reading a book makes them smart. If you are book smart, you'll be alright; street smart, you'll survive the struggle; but to be book and street smart?

Now, that makes you one bad muthafucker!" All the gentlemen *laugh* with Mercandel.

New York asks, "They really believe we are some terrorists?"

Cali carefully explains, "Using intimidation to attain one's goal or to advance one's cause would be terrorism."

New York informs them, "Well, I tap into the I.R.S. Financial database and we are siphoning out their money little by little and they don't even know it. The computers are saying one thing and their stash is going to be saying something else."

Mercandel tells New York, "Set Combs up for the fall."

New York smiles, "Now this is going to be fun."

Florida laughing, "Now that's what in the hell they call terrorism, playing monopoly with the Benjamin's. I have a new chemical I discovered dealing with chromium that will break down the nervous system in less than two seconds. The government would kill to have this one."

Mercandel tells him, "Don't turn that into your supervisors just yet. We may need it."

Cali, amazed, "Wow, that's going to be worth millions, boy you are sharper than a blade."

Florida, quietly, "Thank you brother."

New York smiles.

Detroit, perplexed, "Sir, I don't understand why we just don't take care of the problem. Combs needs to go, no questions asked, just ashes."

Mercandel, calmly, "What problem? I'm a realistic man, and I know hate has brought down nations, kingdoms, fortresses, and homes. Discipline! There is a time for everything, even revenge." Mercandel deliciously eyeballs the shrimp. "I like to serve it cold."

Mercandel then turns his attention to Detroit as he says, "I like the shoes, they complement your suit."

Detroit grins and looks down at his shoe. "Thank you."

Cali glances at Detroit's shoes. "Now that's on time Detroit!" Everyone chuckles.

Everyone continues to eat, but Mercandel notices Detroit's ill behavior at the table. Mercandel asks him, "Is there a problem son?" The others stop eating and look at Detroit.

Mercandel sternly, "And as long as you and I breathe the same air, don't you ever lie to me. My life is an open book. I have ghosts that haunt me everyday I wake up. But they are my ghosts, my troubles, my struggles, not any of yours. I don't hide anything from you."

Cali remarks, "And any son would kill for their father."

Mercandel looks at them all. They turn their heads in different directions. Mercandel laughs sarcastically and strokes his chin. "Okay, I see you all have been talking. Would anyone like to share what they have to say about their feelings?" Mercandel glancing at each in turn, barks "So now we can't talk? We can talk about everything else. But we can't talk about feelings?" Fuming, Mercandel says, "Fine, let's call everything off. You all go your separate directions. It's not too late to start a new life, you all have great jobs."

Cali, looking bewildered, responds "Feelings are for the weak."

Mercandel soberly, "You know, I have feelings. It may be just for five people still left in my life. But never let feelings get in the way of what needs to be and has to be done whatever the situation is. You all thought I came out of a genie bottle?" Mercandel looks up at the ceiling. Mercandel continues, "And I pray to God that you remember I will die for you, so you would live. This is not up for negotiation."

Florida stunned, "If you're all I have, what exactly do you expect for me to do?"

Mercandel responds, "I expect for you to let me die so you all can live."

Florida glances around at the others.

Detroit, upset, "Why are we discussing this?"

Mercandel tacitly, "Let's eat please."

The Glass as one, "Yes Sir."

Total silence at the table.

Mercandel proceeds, "So, I guess because I haven't told you all what you wanted to hear, you are all not going to talk to me...right?" They nod in unison. "That's fine with me. I love you all anyway."

New York keeps his head down. He asks, "Do you really want us to sacrifice the only father we've ever known and will ever know."

Mercandel quietly asks, "So, New York, will you go against my wishes?"

New York looks at Mercandel in his eyes saying, "No, I will not, Sir, because it is your wish."

Mercandel asks, "Then why are we still discussing it?"

Mercandel glances at Cali, "So Cali, do you have a problem or a comment about my decision?"

Cali peers at Mercandel for a good minute without saying a word. "I will respect your wishes Sir, but I'm not sure if I could control my anger after all is said and done."

Mercandel gets up from the table and strolls over to Florida. "Get up son." Florida gets up and Mercandel gives him a hug. Then he gives him a kiss on his forehead. "My wife once told me you get more bees with just basic sweet honey."

Florida responds, "So, what do you do with a wasp?"

Mercandel states, "I love all of you as if you were my sons. Unfortunately, we have to forfeit the game and stick and move. We will meet in Mexico in two months, but everything must go as planned."

Mercandel moseys around the table and kisses each one of them on their forehead and exits the room.

Outside of the cabin Rodrigo stands next to a tree dressed all in black holding a small listening device to his ear and hears Mercandel state "But everything must go as planned."

CHAPTER 20

Rhonda walks into Watkins' office. Watkins drinking coffee looks up to see Rhonda smiling. Watkins with a worried frown asks, "What now, Rhonda?"

Rhonda announces "It looks like we got a break in the case. The owner of the restaurant that blew up last week has surfaced and has identified Mercandel's associates."

Watkins, flustered and confused, "Mercandel? What do you mean Mercandel? How did Mercandel get in the case? Wait, I thought the owner died in the explosion."

Rhonda states, "He was a co-owner."

Watkins demands, "Who are Mercandel's associates?"

Rhonda replies, "Antonio Sanchez, Nathan D'Angelo, Timothy McGee, and Diem Lee. All in their late 20s. They all graduated from Harvard University and all of them have priors." Rhonda takes a deep breath, "I guess your worst nightmare has just come true. Mercandel is back on the move."

Watkins stares at Rhonda thinking. He then starts grabbing papers and writing up paperwork and setting things in place. Watkins barks, "Bring them in for questioning. I want them all in here. And as for the owner, I want him in the witness protection. I want him protected since yesterday."

Rhonda replies, "Sir, we don't know where Mercandel's four accomplices are."

Watkins frantic, "THEN FIND THEM!!! Find them! Find them! I want them all in my interrogation rooms before anything else happens in my city!"

Rhonda replies, "Yes sir."

Watkins finishes filling out a paper and hands it to Rhonda. She takes it and walks out of Watkins' office as he picks up the phone to make a call.

CHAPTER 21

Sky and Mercandel play tennis at the country club in Beverly Hills. Sky hits the ball winning the game. They both sit on a nearby bench. Sky looks into the sky as birds fly by. Sky, apprehensive, "Father, why must I go away again?" She looks at Mercandel. She is persistent "Why must I go away? I want to be with you. I finished school with honors, and you promised me we would be together by now. I have only been home for a week, and you want me to go away again?"

Mercandel looks away momentarily. Mercandel tries reasoning with her, "Sky, I have already explained it to you. The boys and I must take care of some business in a couple of weeks. You can join us in Mexico." He continues softly, "You don't think I will come back for you? Darling, I have never left you."

Tears begin to creep out of Sky's eyes. "It's not fair."

Mercandel hugs Sky. Then he puts his face in the palm of his hands for a minute. Tenderly, he tells her, "I will never leave you; I promise." He takes her face and puts it in the palms of his hands. He gazes into her eyes. "Now, have I ever lied to you?"

Sky, miserable, "No Sir."

Mercandel smiling, "I love you." Mercandel gives her a hug and glances around to see if anyone is watching.

He then warns her, "I do not want you affiliated with Cali, Sky."

Mercandel flashes back to the barbecue at his beach house a few days before where he observed Cali and Sky share a look from across the table. Sky had flirtatiously smiled at Cali who turns his head and focused on something else not sharing the glance. The other members of the Glass are present laughing and talking at the table. Mercandel notices the exchange while grilling the meat. Mercandel shakes his head as he returns to the present.

Sky meekly replies, "Yes Sir."

Mercandel tells her, "You have one life to live. When I adopted you, I gave you another chance. "Mercandel is saddened.

Sky, upset, "God knows my soul hurts for you, Father. In this lifetime, I've already lost one family and you are the only one I have left." She continues, "Do you really want to know why I like him, Father? I like him because he admires you and he is so much like you, a good man." Sky eagerly tells him, "I'm proud of you Father and I think you are a wonderful person." Sky sighs and smiles.

Mercandel gazes at Sky and smiles at her. Then he begins to smirk, laughing underneath his breath. "How long have you been practicing that guilt trip on your Father? Since the day of the barbecue?"

Sky laughs and then suddenly stops. "You know what? You're actually wrong. I did like him, but he reminded me so much of you and the decision you are making will hurt me for the rest of my life. May I be excused?"

Mercandel puts his head down briefly and raises it back up with a smirk guarding his hurt. "You may be excused."

Sky gets up and rushes off MUMBLING something under her breath. Mercandel sits there on the bench smiling with his feet crossed watching Sky storm off.

CHAPTER 22

A few days later Sky stands outside of the Library waiting for Mercandel. She smiles when she sees his Mercedes Benz drive up. She hops in and turns to say hello when she realizes it's Cali. She is annoyed. "Where is my father?"

Cali grimaces and says, I'm sure he'll call and let you know.

Sky, still annoyed, "Look, something has gone wrong with my father and I know you know! My loyalty is not to you, it's to my father. We just so happen to be protecting and loving the same man." Cali drives off slowly as Sky glances at him squinting her eyes with attitude.

Cali states, "You are his daughter. He loves you dearly.

Sky, upset, "Yes, he loves me now by distance. Because he's so much closer to you all as if you were his biological sons, I can tell." She opens her wallet, pulls out a photograph and peers at it. Sky muses as she stares at the picture, "I was supposed to be a surprise for her. I was the most blessed child in the entire world to have such a beautiful family wanting me to be a part of their lives."

Sky looks down at another picture with just Linda and the boys. She continues, "I never got to meet her, but she really could be mistaken as my mother. There was a time when he gave his love freely but since their deaths, you must earn it. I guess that's part of what makes him a great man."

Sky shows Cali a pendant on a chain with the words *My sister forever.* She said, "This necklace was given to me by my brothers." Sadly, She rubbed the pendant gently as she looked at the words engraved on it. "You know my father never missed a birthday or a holiday. Once, I tried to make homemade banana pudding. Well I didn't continue to stir the pan when it was simmering and scorched the bottom which left a burning smell. Needless to say, it didn't taste very good, but my Father ate it anyway." Chuckling at the memory. Sky with a faraway look, "Ever since then, every time he would come visit he would ask for banana pudding and I would make it for him, without burning it."

Tears begin to pour out of her eyes. Sky, weeping silently murmurs, "We are both longing for the same people. We share the same broken heart. All we have is each other." Sky glances at Cali. He drives at a steady pace.

Cali, "That is a blessing."

Sky turning towards Cali as she asks, "Do you know how it feels to wait for something your entire life and lose it all that very same night? I know you know what's going on, but you must protect my father."

The car pulls up slowly in front of Sky's apartment. Cali attempts to get out to open the door for Sky, but she stops him in his tracks. Sky, irritated, "I do not need you to open any door for me. I can do it myself!" Sky gets out of the car and SLAMS the door as hard as one can. Cali rolls down her side of the window as she storms away. He pulls off slowly.

CHAPTER 23

Inside the private interrogation room at the station, The Glass are being questioned. The Special Agents, Combs, Watkins, and other detectives on the case are standing behind the two-way mirror waiting for a break from The Glass. The Glass sits there in two piece suits, sunglasses, and feet crossed totally nonchalant. Combs is getting upset. Inside the waiting area, everyone is looking hopeless.

Combs, resignedly, "They are smart, very, very, smart."

Rhonda says, "They agreed to come in for questioning, but they refuse to answer any questions. She smirks".

One of the Special Agents states, "Because they are literally that shrewd."

Combs glances at his watch and begins to pace the floor. Watkins sits down and sips on his cup of coffee. Combs, angrily, "So we're just going to let them walk out of here tonight! Just walk right out of the door!"

The Special Agent flatly said, "They are innocent until proven guilty."

Combs, bitterly as he flings his arm toward the mirror, "Guilt is written all over their faces!!!" He then turns fully staring at the mirror. Watkins glances at each one of them then back at Combs.

Watkins, resignedly, "I do not see one sign of guilt on any one of their faces."

Rhonda leans on the desk and puts her face in her hands and SIGHS, "Oh my!" Watkins stands up with a SIGH.

The other Special Agent, exasperated, "They are thieves, they are guilty of conspiracy, drug trafficking, and probably human trafficking too. They do it all in their little click with Mr. Wizard telling them how to do it."

Watkins, pissed off said, "We went on a search warrant for Mercandel many years ago-"

Rhonda, interrupting asks, "So what did you find?"

Watkins, continues, "We didn't find what we were expecting to find. We found something that stunned every law enforcement officer in the room."

Watkins strolled over to the mirror and set his gaze on Detroit. The other three are giving their full attention to the interrogators. Detroit slightly turns his head to the mirror and smiles at Watkins.

The nearby Officer blurts out, "Isn't this some shit! He knows you're watching him."

Watkins calmly states, "And they are watching us."

Watkins recalls the day they searched Mercandel's house years ago. *He and the other Officers are searching the house room by room until they get to Mercandel's bedroom. They BURST into the door. The officers are stunned! Watkins, "We went into Mercandel's house and searched his bedroom, which really wasn't a bedroom, but a library of nightmares. The only thing we found in this bedroom of his was one twin bed. Three inches of the wall all the way to the top of the ceiling from all four corners of each wall were covered with every police story, the Constitution, and every law book known to man. He had it in that room. He educated himself like a diabolical mastermind. Mercandel had become the system*

Shaking his head, Watkins shrugs off the memory bringing his focus back to the present and saying "These four are way more dangerous than Mercandel could ever be because they have already been systematized. Mercandel took in all the information and filtered out all the bullshit and spoon fed them straight knowledge."

The Glass has been split up and taken to different Interrogation rooms.

Inside of Interrogation Room 1, the Interrogator asks New York, "Do you need a lawyer?"

Inside of Interrogation Room 2, the Interrogator asks

Florida, "Do you need a lawyer?"

Inside of Interrogation Room 3, the Interrogator asks Cali, "Do you need a lawyer?"

Inside of Interrogation Room 4, the Interrogator asks To Detroit, "Do you need a lawyer?"

Detroit glances at the interrogator and takes off his glasses. Detroit, "Great question. I am a lawyer! I believe since you do not have any evidence to keep us here, I assume that we will be going." Detroit rises and walks out calmly as he meets the others in the hallway.

The Lead Interrogator walks out of the interrogation room to meet up with Combs, Watkins, and Rhonda. He stated, "We have to let them go. Their time is up."

Combs HITS the table with his fist and STORMS out the room. Rhonda sits in a nearby chair and stares up at the ceiling dumbfounded. The Special Agent shakes his head in disbelief as he mutters, "This is unbelievable, absolutely unbelievable. I just don't believe this."

Watkins, with a heavy sigh, "Let them go." The Glass walks out of the police station as some of the police force watch them.

CHAPTER 24

Mercandel walks out of the coffee shop talking on his cell phone with his briefcase in hand. He tells Detroit, "Call the others and let them know that we have to meet at court tomorrow at three o'clock in Los Angeles. It's about time we put an end to this."

The Courtroom is packed. Rodrigo is sitting in the back of the Courtroom. The D.A.'s witness after he is sworn in, glances over at Mercandel and The Glass as he sits down. Suddenly, he jumps out of the chair and begins to frantically feel under the chair *frightened that a bomb is planted under the chair*. He sits back down nervously.

The Glass and Mercandel sit next to Detroit staring at the D.A.'s witness, Mr. James. He is one of the restaurant owner's assistants. Mr. James glanced at his wife and four children nervously.

Detroit said sharply, "Objection! your Honor, the witness cannot testify on something he knows nothing about."

The Judge agrees, "Overruled!"

The D.A. stands up continuing to question the witness, "Mr. James, we have pictures of the six of you together. You, the deceased Mr. Hunt, and these four men. So, you do know or have some type of affiliation with Mr. Mercandel, Mr. Lee, Mr. Sanchez, Mr. McGee and Mr. D'Angelo?"

Mr. James, frightened, thinking back to the day he was brought in for questioning and the deal he was offered.

The D.A., Combs and Rhonda were taking his statement. The D.A. tells him,. "The charges they face automatically incriminates you as an accomplice. Today, the plea we are offering you is to spend the rest of your life in jail or testify against them and walk out of here a free man. You have a decision to make today Mr. James! Your wife, children and your life depend on it. Mr. James, you do want your family and your life back, don't you?"

The D.A., loudly, "Mr. James" startling the witness and bringing his focus back to the courtroom. "Please answer the question"

Mercandel and The Glass have their eyes totally focused on Mr. James causing him to be jittery. As he hesitates to answer, the D.A. turns to the Judge pointing a finger at Mercandel and The Glass as he exclaims, "Your Honor, they are intimidating my witness."

Detroit calmly, "Your honor. This is a free country. My

clients are only paying attention to the charges that have been falsely brought against them."

The courtroom erupts in angry mummers and some chuckling. The judge HITS his gavel on the bench as he thunders "Order in the courtroom! Overruled."

Mr. James still in the witness chair continues to shake nervously. Mercandel rubs his hands together slowly while looking at Mr. James.

The D.A. continuing, "Were you his associate by choice or because you feared him so much, you preferred to be on his good side as a friend?"

Detroit, standing, "Objection! Speculation."

Judge, "SUSTAINED."

The D.A. doggedly continues to question Mr. James, "Were you leaving the scene after Mr. Sanchez left the restaurant on November twenty-third, approximately fifteen minutes prior to the bombing?" Mr. James looks at the Glass and then looks down as he answers "Yes I was."

The D.A. turns to the courtroom and jury as he states, "Anyone who sits here in this courtroom today will not believe that you do not even know these men," pointing at Mercandel and The Glass.

Detroit, strongly, "Objection! Leading the witness."

Judge, "Sustained"

The D.A. is getting agitated. He turns back to the witness stating, "There were cameras inside. Wouldn't they be working 24/7 in a successful restaurant. Then, the cameras were just shut down on Tuesday at twelve for a half hour every month., which is strange for a restaurant bringing in that type of money and business. The defendants held a meeting plotting the bombing." Mercandel sits with a smug look.

Detroit, jumps up, "Objection! Speculation."

The Judge never takes his eyes off of the D.A. and Mr. James. Mercandel leans back and stares at Mr. James.

Mr. James has another flashback to the interrogation room as he remembers the D.A., Combs, and Rhonda were in the room taking his statement. The D.A. said "I just can't believe the restaurant does not have any type of cameras inside and out, which is very strange for a restaurant bringing in that type of money. You had to have seen something because, if not, it's just the same as you blowing up the restaurant yourself. We know there were no chemicals on your prints or clothing. Those types of chemicals can only be produced by some type of genius

Mr. James nervously shakes away the memory. The D.A. bluntly states, "Unfortunately, the other witnesses are dead. They were all blown up in a thousand and two pieces...except you! He pauses to let the horror of what happened sink in and then continues, "Which we now know, whether you believe it or not, is the aftermath of Mercandel and the young gentlemen referred to as The Glass. You are the only one who can bring justice to the innocent people who were killed and their families."

Mr. James still trembling is totally silent. He glances at everyone in the courtroom before looking at the D.A. and blurts out "I will do life!"

A couple of reporters are taking pictures as the courtroom erupts in outrage and a lot of mumbling and whispers at what they just heard.

The Judge takes off his GLASSES striking the podium with his gravel as he yells "Order in the courtroom! Order!"

Detroit, standing, "Your Honor, I motion that the case be dismissed for lack of evidence."

Judge, concurs, "Motion Granted. Case Dismissed" The Judge strikes his gavel as he says "Court is Adjourned.

CHAPTER 25

Inside of the police station Combs, Rhonda, Watkins, detectives and other policemen are watching the news of the case and are making plans on how to trick Mercandel.

Rhonda, dismayed at what happened at the trial states, "One of them will break."

COMBS distressed; asks, "How do you break something that's already been broken?"

Rhonda responds, "We have never attempted. They are playing us at our own game, and they are winning."

Another Detective with a heavy sigh, "They have already won."

Watkins, disturbed, "That's exactly why the mafia has hired him, because of his ability to be inconspicuous." Watkins raises up a PICTURE OF MERCANDEL. "Who does he look like to you? Stop looking at the innocent, calm look! The day his family was murdered was the day he became a threat to the entire world."

Combs angrily, "If you do not catch all four at one time, it's going to be some shit. Those young men would blow up the entire United States if needed to free this one man."

Watkins turns to Rhonda, "Gather up everyone's report, we are going to get them."

Rhonda, eagerly "Yes Sir."

Everyone begins to scramble. Rhonda stays behind to talk to Watkins and Combs. She boldly states, "We need to set up near their home. If possible, sit across the street from only one of them, the one that feels he has intimidated us with his half-crooked smile. He takes trips on business at least five times out of the month. From the pictures to the cookie jars, break them down to nothing and fix everything back all the way to the candy wrapper on his rug. That is the only way we will find something on them. We are going to have to become illegal."

Watkins, emphatically, "We can't do that Rhonda. This entire police station could be shut down if we get caught up in illegal activity. "

Rhonda walks over to Watkins. She states, "So we won't get caught!"

Combs replies, Then we need to go in and find something because he's sure too damn smart for us to plant something! Let's get the search warrant."

Watkins looks up at the news as Mr. James yells, "I will do life." Watkins turns to Rhonda. "Well, it's a go, but our shit needs to be cleaned up like using sandpaper to wipe a monkey's ass. "

Rhonda, "Thank you Sir." She starts to walk out of the room.

Watkins, quietly, "The best, Rhonda." Rhonda turns around slowly as Watkins repeats, "The best, Rhonda."

Rhonda turns around slowly with a sense of confidence and exclaims, "Yes Sir!"

CHAPTER 26

The entire law enforcement team on the case moves in quietly across the street from New York's house. cameras with telescopes are secretly installed in the windows. TVs are set up with monitors in the house. Rhonda and Combs wait anxiously looking out the window. New York's CAR pulls out of the driveway. Rhonda paces the floor with a cup of coffee in her hand.

Combs walks over to her. "You will get the Badge of Honor if you can catch one of them."

Rhonda stops in her tracks and smiles. "Do you feel it's impossible?"

Combs replies, "No, I do not feel it is impossible, but I'm glad that you will get the recognition you deserve."

Rhonda, exhaling deeply, "You just remember; innocent until proven guilty."

Combs laughs to himself. "You wanna know why I'm still on the case Rhonda? Because I have been the only one to get close enough to catching Mercandel."

Rhonda smiles, "Really?! Close enough doesn't count in the real world." Another detective walks up to Rhonda and Combs as Combs' cell phone rings. He looks at the number strangely before answering it.

Rodrigo gruffly asks, "You want him bad don't you?"

Combs, mystified, "Who is this?"

Rodrigo replies, "Just someone who wants Mercandel just as bad as you. Three of the boys are already gone."

Combs walks away from Rhonda as he demands, "Gone where? Where?"

Rodrigo tells him, "That is of no importance to me. My vendetta is not against the boys or his daughter, unlike you. Your bullet or mine, my superior wants him down." There is a DIAL TONE. Combs slowly walks over to Rhonda.

One of the detectives whispers, "Detective Rhonda, he's about to leave."

Rhonda, nervous, "Here we go, ready or not."

Combs responds, "This will be a piece of pie."

Rhonda stares at the detectives standing there anxious. Rhonda pointing out the window, "Follow him. WE NEED TIME! We need to be able to go in and search that house inside and out. And we can't do that until we get time. "

Combs' phone rings. He answers, "Okay, thank you." Combs then rushes off in a hurry, but quickly turns to address Rhonda, "Today is your lucky day. He just drove into the airport parking lot. The world is cold, but it's fair." The forensics team starts to collect their suitcases. Everyone puts on GLOVES and PLASTIC SHOE COVERS. They wait at the door for the word to exit the house. Rhonda's phone rings as Combs walks up.

RHONDA (on the phone) "You need to make sure someone is there from the time that plane touches down in Vegas until I say to pull back. I need to know the color of his shit if I need to." Rhonda turns to Combs.

A FBI AGENT approaches Rhonda and Combs stating, It's a go. This job must be clean." The Forensics Team goes into New York's home first taking pictures of everything showing the placement of a paper on the table to the angles of the pictures on the wall. *This is to help them to put everything back exactly as they found it.*

The rest of the team enters and begins a thorough search of the house. This goes on for two days, but nothing is found.

Rhonda sits outside with a cup of coffee. Combs walks over to her bewildered, "Nothing. Not a damn thing!!!"

Rhonda gazes at the large pond that sits in the backyard. She states, "We need to step up our game. Call the search off. Somehow, I feel they are laughing and watching us right now as we speak."

Combs, bitterly, "I told you to ambush, kill them, and

then ask questions later...DAMN!!!"

Rhonda calmly looks at him and said, "And I will be the one to turn you in regardless of what's going on, this is still America. Our job is to arrest the criminals and make sure the evidence is beyond circumstantial, not just go around shooting people because we can't do our job and find a cause."

Combs, simmering, "It's been two days. Remember, this was your idea."

Rhonda glares at Combs as she rises and gets in his face, "And as long as I'm on this case, I will be watching you and any other law enforcement officers for any loopholes or death traps you may try to use illegally to catch them. When we find them guilty, we will bring them in."

Combs steps up to Rhonda and lowers his voice, "This whole plan, your plan, is illegal. Don't forget that. A pregnant pause."

Rhonda lowers her voice warning, "If you go down, I am NOT going down with you!" Rhonda storms outside. Tables, glass, and furniture are replaced carefully by the forensic team using the pictures taken earlier to help them put everything exactly like it was.

Rhonda's cell phone rings and she answers, "What? I thought he wasn't coming back until Thursday! Dammit!!!"

Rhonda gazes at their equipment on the ground. RHONDA frantically yelling, "We got to get this up and back in, people! He's on his way back!"

Everyone grabs equipment quickly and runs inside.

Back in the house across the street, Rhonda and Combs stare out the window at New York as he drives up. When New York gets out of his car, he glances across the street. Rhonda ducks.

Combs says, He can't see us."

Rhonda, quietly, "Yeah, just in case."

New York walks inside.

That night the entire police force exhausted has fallen asleep. Suddenly, there are loud noises. The officers jump up with their guns. A DVD playing on TV shows themselves illegally searching through New York's house. Rhonda and Combs watch it in awe.

Combs LAUGHS and then says "And y'all said not to kill them. A joke! We could be dead right now!" He then turns to Rhonda, "When my opportunity comes, I will take advantage of it and you just make sure you are not in the way." Combs STORMS off.

The police force is loading their equipment in vans. New York faces the house across the street as he sits comfortably in a rocking chair on his porch. He is drinking coffee and reading a newspaper. He never looks up or over at the detectives as they load their equipment in the van. Rhonda stops and stares at New York as she struggles to put one of the suitcases in the van.

Combs LAUGHS as he moseys towards Rhonda. Rhonda glared at him, saying, "Get out of my face!"

Everyone gets in the vans. They watch New York on his porch as they drive off.

CHAPTER 27

Rodrigo, on his cell phone, answers "I'm following his daughter now. I will catch both of them alone without the boys. I have an inside connection with the police, a Detective Combs who tried to bring him down the first time. Today will be the day. She will lead me to Mercandel."

Sky speeds down I-10 in the direction of her father's house. Her phone rings. Sky answers. "Father, where have you been? I've been calling and calling. "

Mercandel tells her, "Listen to me and listen to me well. We can't talk on this phone, it's tapped. But we only have three minutes before they can trace this call. There's a note in your glove compartment. Follow exactly what it tells you. I love you so much more than you may know."

Sky is in tears. She responds, "Yes, Father."

Mercandel, "I will be there in a couple of hours." Mercandel laughing, "I better have that banana pudding waiting for me."

Sky, smiling said, "Father I love you so very much, so very much."

Mercandel, tenderly, "I know you do Tinker Bell." Then he commands her "HANG UP NOW!"

Sky hangs up the phone. She pulls over to the nearest gas station and takes out the note hearing her father's voice as she reads "Tinker Bell, there has been a change of plans. A car is awaiting your arrival, the keys are underneath the seat at Fifth Avenue on the side of the Pizza Parlor. Your tickets for the plane will be in the glove compartment. There's a lot of clothes in your trunk that I know you will look nice in. Daddy picked them out himself. Whatever you do, keep your glasses on. There's a wig for your hair. When you get a couple of blocks from the airport, catch a cab. Whatever you do Sky, do not miss that plane. Don't wait for me, I will meet you there in Mexico City. Love Dad."

Sky speeds out of the gas station parking lot.

CHAPTER 28

It's very quiet in the police station. Combs walks around the room handing out papers, starting with Rhonda. Officers begin to read.

Watkins begins, "We suspect that there are bugs in the office, so as a precaution we will be briefed on paper today, so the operation isn't blown. Everyone begins to read:

> *Mercandel's adopted daughter's name is Sky. She left boarding school a couple of weeks ago and is now in California. There was a ticket purchased a few hours ago under her name for Mexico City. The plane will take off in an hour. I believe all the members of the Glass have already landed in Mexico City within the pass week. Now, she is the bait. She may not know anything. The nuns say she's very timid. Mercandel and Sky are going to try to get on this next flight.*

Several look up at Watkins. He nods for them to continue reading.

He will not take a chance of leaving her behind, I'm certain they will get on the plane together. We need to head to the airport now. We will have a photocopy of that young lady for everyone in a few minutes. Watkins raises his hands. Everyone is to grab their GUNS AND GEAR and head for the airport.

Suddenly, FBI Agents come bursting through the door. One of them grabs Combs by his shirt saying "You are under arrest. You are charged with electronically robbing several State National Banks for the grand total of $500 Million. You have the right to remain silent, anything you say or do will be..."

Combs jerks away violently demanding, "What are you talking about? Get the fuck off of me! Are you out of your mind? I don't even have a bank account!"

The FBI Agent replies, "That's exactly what we are saying. What are you doing in the bank with a checkbook? Not just this one..." He pulls out a FILE with copies of checks pointing as he says "This one....this one...and this one and about six more."

Combs turning to Watkins angrily yelling, "They framed me! They are trying to leave the country! They are at the airport!"

The FBI Agent states, "We have solid proof of what we need to place you under arrest."

Watkins walks over to the FBI Agent. Suddenly, Combs

RUNS past the FBI Agents and out the door. The agents draw their weapons and pursue Detective Combs.

CHAPTER 29

Sky arrives at the airport terminal and checks her bags in at the check-in in front of the terminal. She then parks the car. Wearing ROUND-FACED GLASSES and a WIG, she heads back to the terminal

Mercandel and Cali are at the graveyard standing side by side peering down at the tombstones of Mercandel's wife and children. Mercandel, softly, "Well my beautiful black butterfly, I'm about to leave the states for good, and of course I'm taking Sky with me." Cali turns his head away. Mercandel lays down a dozen of ROSES on his wife's grave.

Cali quietly, "We must go now, Sir."

Mercandel looks up at Cali. "Yeah, it's time for us to go now." Mercandel and Cali walk off. Mercandel gets into his car and Cali gets into the waiting taxi.

Sky is standing in line noticing detectives in the crowds. Combs passes right beside her and stops. Combs speaking into a walkie talkie. "I'm taking him down."

Combs puts the walkie talkie back in his coat pocket. He accidentally knocks Sky's cell phone out of her hands. He picks it up and looks up at her. Combs politely, "Excuse me Ma'am, I'm very sorry."

Sky (Spanish) "Oh gracias. Tener un buen día."

Combs smiles and hands her the phone that has Mercandel as the wallpaper on the screen. Then he walks off. He stops. A beat. He turns around and Sky is gone. He starts looking for her. Sky hides in an old janitor's room, but too far away from her terminal.

Combs calls Rhonda yelling into the walkie talkie, "She's here. I just picked up her phone and it wasn't even two minutes and she vanished."

Rhonda responds, "Then where is she? The FBI is looking for you. "

Combs, looking around, "I'm not sure, but I am looking for her. I don't want to draw too much attention to myself because I think she is watching me. I don't think she will leave without her father though."

Combs, continuing to search, tells Rhonda, "Notify your men." He continues to scan the area for Sky.

Arriving at the airport, Mercandel gets out of his car handing the keys to the valet parking attendant. A taxi is dropping off Cali nearby. Mercandel and Cali dressed in three-piece tailored suits stroll into the airport from two different entrances.

Rodrigo stands against the wall near the entrance Mercandel enters. Mercandel walks right past him. Rodrigo follows him. Cali and Mercandel walk perpendicular to each other. Mercandel notices the crowd moving awkwardly. He sees Combs from a distance. Rodrigo follows Mercandel with a Nine Millimeter at his side. Cali sees Rodrigo and picks up his pace. He quickly loads his gun and holds it down along the side of his leg as he continues toward Rodrigo. A split second before reaching Rodrigo his gun fully loaded, he sees Rodrigo raising his gun aiming at Mercandel's head. In a blink of an eye, Cali raises his gun, pulls the trigger shooting Rodrigo in the head not even bothering to watch him fall as he joins Mercandel in the same walking pace without skipping a beat and not drawing attention to himself.

At the sound of the gunshot, people start SCREAMING and running. Cali and Mercandel are keeping their eyes on Combs. Mercandel tells Cali, "Turn and walk."

Cali turns an about face without hesitation. Mercandel continues to walk in Combs' direction. Combs still doesn't see him yet, but Sky does.

She HISSES, "Father, Father." Mercandel ignores Sky calling him. She is overwhelmed as she watches Mercandel move closer to Combs. Sky upset, whispers, "What are you doing? What are you doing!?!"

Sky creeps into Combs' line of vision. Combs glances

at Sky, sees Mercandel and smiles. Mercandel stops in front of Combs. The other detectives arrest Sky. She doesn't resist and puts her hands out in front of her body, and they HANDCUFF her.

Mercandel asks, "May I call my lawyer please? You didn't give me that opportunity the first time."

A detective holds Sky's arm as they escort her closer to Combs and Mercandel.

Combs sarcastically, "You really went out of your way to protect and hide your little princess, Sky." Combs turns to Sky who stands with her head down. She is crying.

Rhonda and Watkins further down are struggling to get past the running, screaming crowd to get to Combs and Mercandel.

Rhonda yelling into her walkie talkie "Don't you dare do anything stupid. Hold him until the Lieutenant and I get there. COMBS, DON'T YOU DARE, WE ARE ON OUR WAY!" Rhonda turns her head to Watkins saying, "We better hurry."

Sky meekly, "Father, I'm so sorry."

Mercandel gazes at Sky with a smile, telling her, "Don't you dare cry Sky."

Combs walks over to Sky sarcastically, "Yeah, don't cry Sky."

Sky looks up slowly at Combs with tears in her eyes,

whispers, "Loyalty is priceless and love can't be bought or negotiated!"

Combs turns back to Mercandel very angry. "You have all of them brainwashed. I mean really, how do you do that shit? I mean, she's about to do life with you and she's talking about love and loyalty."

Mercandel asks "Was starting over rough?"

Combs, startled, "What the fuck did you just say?"

Mercandel has a smirk on his face. Combs walks up closer to Mercandel and puts his finger to Mercandel's head, "I'm going to get inside of your head."

Mercandel points at his own head with a smirk said slowly emphasizing each word, "I. THREW. AWAY. THE. KEY."

Combs raises his gun and shoots Mercandel in the head. Combs puts the gun back in his holster as he stands over Mercandel and watches.

Chaos erupts all around Sky as she stands there in shock. She begins to CRY, "Father, please don't leave me!"

The crowd is SCREAMING and running.

Sky in shock grabs a GUN out of the detective's holster next to her as she remembers:

She is about 13 or 14 lying in the grass back in Africa taking aim at three gazelles as Abel her trainer whispers in her ear "breathe silently, slow it down, then take aim. Do not blink until you have taken them all down. You have one bullet for each...take them all down in the rhythm of one breath"

Sky takes a deep breath calmly taking aim to shoot him in the head. Without missing a beat, she shoots the four other detectives who were between her and Combs in the back of their heads and watches as they fall one after another. Sky then makes eye contact with Combs. He backs up and attempts to pull his gun from the holster. Sky is steadily walking up to him, She bitterly says, "This is for my brothers and mother." Sky SHOOTS him in the chest. Detective Combs falls to his knees. "And this is for my father She SHOOTS him in the neck. "And this, this is for me." She SHOOTS him in the forehead. Detective Combs falls backwards lifelessly onto the floor.

Watkins and Rhonda arrive on the scene in total shock. Sky, in handcuffs, is crying and holding Mercandel tightly.

About the author

Epic Sky was born in New Orleans. She attributes her writing talents to her eldest sister Diane Brown who inspired her at the age of sixteen to write her first script.

She earned the locals' attention as a first-time producer and promoter with her nonprofit stage play, *I've Done My Share and Then Some*, in 2003 that was performed for former Mayor of New Orleans Marc Morial and the United Teachers Union of New Orleans. She was recognized as one of New Orleans finest amateurs. The play recognition gave her and her cast an invitation to perform later at McDonald 35 Magnet High School and a host of other public schools.

She hosted her own poetry spot in the heart of the Crescent City. Later on, winning the Def Jam's Poet Competition and was invited to perform at Chris Tucker Joint in Atlanta, on Peachtree Blvd.

For the next couple of years until the devastation of Katrina. Epic Sky had her own successful business, Thoughts Inside of a Picture. She would put people's heart-felt feelings soaked in words of inspirational poetry onto their most treasured pictures. This business by itself opened a new social world of opportunities. Although, she lost all her contacts when Hurricane Katrina hit New Orleans, she never lost her hope, dreams and faith to become one of the world's greatest screenwriters. She only escaped Katrina with her USB drive around her neck that contained her greatest life admiration's. For months she wrote on tablets that she saved up daily. She says, "Starting over is not such a bad thing. It's in what frame of mind you are starting over with."

Her Scripts include: *Slippery Glass, Clean, 3 oz, L.E.A.S.A., Down O.G's Get Down, Free, Don't Take The Short Cut Home, I've Done My Share and Then Some, The Tree, The Corner Store, Faithful*, and many more. Watch for my upcoming sequeal in the continuing story of Slippery Glass called *Hades*.

She has also written and published several books: *The Stain of a Black Man, The Depth of a Soul Sistaz's Inner Thoughts*, and *Nurturing to a Woman's Inner Peace*. They were sold out at every poetry reading she hosted or performed once a week at Pal's, Hard Rock Cafe and Ebony's Corner.